Maybe the sheik was right. . . .

They did a scan of my head and shoulder at the hospital. The doctor said my helmet did its job protecting me, but my shoulder took a beating. He asked about the old fracture from when I came off Honor at the Whitebrook practice track. I told him that was years ago. He said breaks heal, but without proper therapy and rest, damaged tendons and ligaments have to be repaired surgically. He said if I don't treat my shoulder right, I could end up crippled. I don't know what to do anymore. I've only managed to ride in two races since I've been at Belmont, and they've both been terrible. Maybe the sheik was right all along. I have no talent. I've just been lucky. Until now.

Collect all the books in the Thoroughbred series

THOROUGHBRED Super Editions
Ashleigh's Christmas Miracle
Ashleigh's Diary
Ashleigh's Hope
Samantha's Journey

ASHLEIGH'S Thoroughbred Collection
Star of Shadowbrook Farm
The Forgotten Filly
Battlecry Forever!

* coming soon

THOROUGHBRED

CINDY'S BOLD START

CREATED BY
JOANNA CAMPBELL

WRITTEN BY
MARY NEWHALL ANDERSON

HarperEntertainment
An Imprint of HarperCollinsPublishers

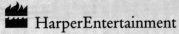

HarperEntertainment

An Imprint of HarperCollins*Publishers*
10 East 53rd Street, New York, NY 10022-5299

This is a work of fiction. The characters, incidents, and dialogues are products of the author's imagination and are not to be construed as real. Any resemblance to actual events or persons, living or dead, is entirely coincidental.

Produced by 17th Street Productions, an Alloy Online, Inc., company

HarperCollins books are available at special quantity discounts for bulk purchases for sales promotions, premiums, or fund-raising. For information please call or write: Special Markets Department, HarperCollins Publishers Inc., 10 East 53rd Street, New York, NY 10022. Telephone: (212) 207-7528. Fax: (212) 207-7222.

ISBN 0-06-106822-5

First printing: August 2001

Printed in the United States of America

Visit HarperEntertainment on the World Wide Web at www.harpercollins.com

❖ 10 9 8 7 6 5 4 3 2 1

For Meghan, Matthew, Kacie, Ryan, Danielle, Chris, Patrick, Leah, Luke, and Janet

"STERLING SURE LOOKS GOOD," CINDY MCLEAN SAID, watching her sister, Samantha Nelson, take the gray Thoroughbred mare over a jump. Cindy was standing with Christina Reese near the arena fence at Whisperwood, the training facility owned by Samantha and her husband, Tor Nelson. As a jockey, Cindy knew very little about jumping and dressage, but she was impressed with how skillfully her sister handled the energetic mare.

Cindy shivered a little and shoved her hands deep into her pockets. The weather was pleasant for early February, but standing in the cool air didn't do much to keep her warm. She should be riding, too. But according to her doctor, Cindy wouldn't be getting back on a horse for several more weeks, and never again as a jockey. She'd better get used to watching other people do what she loved.

Beside Cindy, Christina Reese applauded when Samantha and Sterling completed another jump. Christina's parents, Ashleigh Griffen and Mike Reese, owned Whitebrook, the nearby Thoroughbred farm where both Cindy and Samantha had grown up. Cindy shot a glance at the seventeen-year-old. An avid three-day-event rider, Christina had surprised everyone when she turned her focus to racing and sold her eventing mare, Sterling Dream, to Samantha. Christina had gotten her jockey's license the previous spring and started working intensely with Wonder's Star, an outstanding three-year-old Thoroughbred that she owned with her parents.

"Sammy can sure make Sterling fly," Christina said, nodding in approval as the mare soared easily over a four-foot wall, making Samantha's long braid of red hair bounce when they landed.

Cindy reached up to touch her own close-cropped blond hair. Keeping it short had been convenient when she was a jockey. But now that her career had ended, she could let her hair grow as long as she wanted. She smiled thinly. That was one positive aspect of being unable to race anymore. There had to be some other good things, but Cindy hadn't discovered them yet.

Cindy turned away from the arena to look more closely at Christina. The girl had been just four when Cindy left Kentucky at eighteen, but now Christina was several inches taller than Cindy. Her strawberry blond hair had darkened to a red-brown color that reminded Cindy of a chestnut Thoroughbred's shiny coat. The cold air had reddened her cheeks, and she was smiling as she watched Samantha canter Sterling around the arena.

"Do you miss jumping like that?" Cindy asked her.

"Not at all," Christina said, shaking her head firmly. She swept a strand of loose hair away from her face with a gloved hand. "I love riding Star and being on the track. It would be horrible if I couldn't race." She snapped her mouth shut and gave Cindy an apologetic look. "Sorry," she said, biting at her lip. "I didn't mean . . ."

Cindy smiled and shrugged. "It's okay, Chris," she said, patting the girl's shoulder. "I'm all right with it. I've had a good career as a jockey. It just ended a little sooner than I thought it would."

After years of repeated stress and injuries, surgery had failed to restore Cindy's damaged left shoulder to full use. Forced to accept the fact that she would never again be fit to race, Cindy had decided to put her experience to use as a racehorse trainer.

"When are you going to move over to Tall Oaks?"

Christina asked. Cindy had been staying at White-brook, where her stepfather, Ian McLean, worked as the head trainer. She had recently taken a job with Fredericka Graber, who had a breeding farm near Whitebrook.

"I need to go up to Elmont and clean out my apartment," Cindy said. "When I get back from New York, I'll move all my stuff into Fredericka's guest house and start my new job."

"Would you like me to go to New York with you?" Christina offered. "I could miss a couple of days of school without any problem."

"That's really sweet of you, Chris," Cindy said, touched by the offer. Since her return to Lexington the previous fall, Cindy knew, she had been pretty hard to get along with. But in spite of her moodiness, her family and old friends had stood by her, and that meant a lot to Cindy. "I can't imagine you'd want to be stuck in the car for hours with an old grouch like me, though."

Christina laughed. "Every time I see you around the horses, I realize that the whole grouch thing is just an act. Underneath it all you're a big softie."

Cindy widened her eyes in mock alarm. "You're not going to tell anyone, are you?"

"Your secret is safe with me," Christina said, pressing her finger to her lips. "But I'd still be happy to help you clean out your apartment."

4

"I really appreciate the offer, but I'll be fine," Cindy said. "I haven't got much stuff. It won't take long to get it all packed."

She turned toward the arena again as Samantha stopped Sterling and hopped from the mare's back.

Samantha grinned at Cindy and Christina. "She's such a great horse," she said, petting the mare fondly.

"I know," Christina said, rubbing Sterling's nose.

Cindy watched them fuss over the mare, a tiny smile tugging at the corners of her mouth. She was more no-nonsense about horses than Samantha or Christina, but she understood how they felt. To have the trust of such a big, powerful animal was an incredible feeling.

Cindy thought back to the last several years, when she had been a jockey at the Belmont racetrack. She remembered riding a Whitebrook filly, Honor Bright, in the Gazelle at Belmont when she first got her jockey's license. For a moment Cindy could once again feel the sun on her face, hear the sounds of the horses in the starting gate on either side of her, sense the excitement of the fans gathered at the rail. She could feel the coiled energy building in the chestnut filly as Honor anticipated the moment the gate would fly open and they would explode onto the track. But even while waiting tensely for the start of the race, Honor listened as Cindy spoke softly, reassuring the excited filly that she would guide her safely through the crowded field and over the finish line ahead of the others. Cindy gave her head a quick shake. She had better get used to the fact that all of this was in her past.

Samantha smiled at her. "I'm glad you've decided to stay in Kentucky, Cindy," she said. "We'll finally be able to spend some time together."

Cindy nodded. Samantha was several years older than Cindy, so the girls hadn't spent a lot of time together when they were younger. Sam had moved to Ireland with Tor when Cindy was in high school, and shortly after she turned eighteen, Cindy had accompanied Whitebrook's Triple Crown-winning stallion, Wonder's Champion, to his new owners' villa in Dubai. After several months in the Middle East, Cindy had returned to the United States to make her mark on the racing world at Belmont. In the last twelve years she hadn't made many visits home. Now it looked as though she was going to have a lot of time to spend with her family.

She glanced at her watch. "It's getting late," she said. "I need to head back to Whitebrook. I still have to call the moving company and my landlord this afternoon. I'm leaving early tomorrow for New York."

"I'm going to stick around here," Christina said, taking Sterling's reins while Samantha pulled the mare's saddle from her back. "Parker will be coming by in a little while to teach a lesson. I'll get a ride home from him."

Parker Townsend, Christina's boyfriend, worked

as an instructor at Whisperwood and boarded his eventing mare, Foxy Miss, there.

"I'll see you later, then," Cindy said, heading for her car, which was parked near Whisperwood's boarding barn.

A few minutes later she turned her car onto the Whitebrook drive, stopping at the entrance to the farm for a moment to look over the familiar setting. She was still trying to get used to the fact that she was back where she had started. Although the old farmhouse where the Reeses lived looked much the same as it had when Cindy came to Whitebrook as a young orphan, the barns had been expanded. Mike and Ashleigh were typical horse people, improving the horse facilities before spending money on their own house. Cindy nodded in approval. If she had her own farm, she would do things exactly the same way.

She drove past the barns to the McLeans' cottage, and dialed Fredericka Graber's number as soon as she got inside. She wanted to talk to her new boss about some ideas she had for making improvements to the stallion barn at Tall Oaks. But when she got Fredericka's answering machine, Cindy hung up. She'd have plenty of time later to go over the changes she hoped to make. Instead she put her restless energy to good use, cleaning up her room and getting the few things she had brought with her from New York packed and ready to take to Fredericka's. After a quiet evening with her family, she went to bed early, and woke the next morning before daylight to start her drive northeast to New York.

When Cindy had left her apartment the previous fall, she had been sure it was only going to be for a short time. But when the surgeon in Lexington informed her that racing again was out of the question unless she wanted to risk permanent injury to her shoulder, she had been devastated. For a while she moped around Whitebrook, depressed and irritable, trying to deal with the end of her racing career.

Then she had been offered the job at Tall Oaks. One of Fredericka Graber's colts, Gratis, was a Kentucky Derby contender, so even if Cindy never got to race in the Kentucky Derby, at least she could be part of it. Along with managing Tall Oaks and all the horses there, Cindy would be the assistant trainer to Vince Jones, who was in charge of Gratis's conditioning. Cindy looked forward to working with the famous trainer and building her own reputation as a trainer.

After spending the night in a motel near Pittsburgh, Pennsylvania, Cindy woke up at dawn the next day to finish the drive to Elmont. As she got close to New York, Cindy found her upbeat mood fading. Coming back into the city brought back a fresh flood of memories. For several years she had been one of the most popular jockeys at the Belmont racetrack. Now she was an ex-jockey and would never again experience the thrill of breaking from the gate astride a racing Thoroughbred. Cindy exhaled heavily and followed the familiar route to Elmont, where the track and her apartment were located.

When she reached the turnoff to the track, Cindy caught herself taking the exit out of habit. There were no races being run at Belmont right now. The only people at the track would be a few trainers and grooms. But she parked at the track's backside lot and got out of the car anyway.

The security guard at the back gate waved her through, and Cindy headed for the shed rows, where the Thoroughbreds were stabled.

She passed a few occupied stalls, but for the most part the barns were quiet, void of the flurry of activity that filled the area during the racing season.

"Cindy!"

When she heard her name, Cindy turned to see a dark-haired woman hurrying toward her.

"Rachel!" she exclaimed, giving the other woman a quick hug in greeting. When Cindy had first moved to Belmont, Rachel Daniels was her best friend and roommate. Rachel's husband, Matt McGrady, had been the first trainer to give Cindy a job, and she had remained friends with the couple over the years.

"You've come back for good now, right?" the other

jockey asked, stepping back to eye Cindy. "Is your shoulder back to normal? Please say yes. It just hasn't been the same here without you."

Cindy felt her smile slip away. "No," she said. "Actually, I'm grounded for good. No more racing for me."

Rachel's jaw dropped and her eyes widened. "Oh, Cindy," she exclaimed. "That's awful. After all your hard work. It isn't fair!"

"I'll be okay," Cindy said firmly. "I took a job in Kentucky. I'm going to be a trainer at Tall Oaks."

"Tall Oaks?" Rachel repeated. "Isn't that the stable that owns Gratis? I exercised him for Vince Jones one time. What a nightmare!"

"He was in the money when Christina Reese rode him here last fall," Cindy countered. Christina had gained the colt's confidence and taken him from being a troublemaker on the track to a winning racehorse. But Christina had her own Derby contender, Wonder's Star, to work with. Vince Jones felt Gratis needed a firmer hand than Christina could manage for his off-track training. The headstrong colt was still difficult to deal with, but Cindy was sure she could bring him around without breaking his fiery spirit.

Rachel nodded. "I saw that race. Gratis can run, I'll give him that. But he's got enough attitude for two horses."

Cindy nodded. "Getting him to be consistent is going to be one of my little projects," she said.

10

Rachel nodded. "If anyone can bring a problem horse around, you can," she said. "You'll be a great trainer."

"Thanks," Cindy said. "Speaking of trainers, how's your husband?"

"Matt's terrific," Rachel replied. "Do you have time to stop by our stalls and see him?"

"I only have a few minutes," Cindy said. "I need to get over to the apartment and start packing."

"Remember when you moved into that place with me?" Rachel asked. "It's strange to think you won't be living there anymore."

"I never did like the view anyway," Cindy said with a chuckle.

Rachel laughed. "No, you always complained about looking out at a brick wall. But even when you could have afforded a better view, you never moved."

"I got used to it," Cindy said, shrugging. "Besides, I spent most of my time here. I only ate and slept at the apartment."

After a brief visit to Matt and Rachel's Stone Ridge Stables, Cindy left the track. She drove slowly through the city, reluctant to face her apartment, where she would have to pack up twelve years of her life into cardboard boxes and ship them to Kentucky.

When she finally opened the apartment door, she stuck her head inside and sniffed the air cautiously.

She had left on the spur of the moment, not expecting to be gone for months. To Cindy's relief, the only scent she could detect was lemon-scented cleaner. She flipped on the lights and dragged the pile of cardboard boxes she had lugged upstairs from her car into the narrow entryway.

The tiny hall table was stacked with neat piles of mail, but the table had been dusted, and when she walked into the little living room, the carpet showed signs of recent vacuuming. She opened the refrigerator, prepared to see an array of moldy food, but the only thing on the shelves was a box of baking soda, meant to keep the refrigerator smelling fresh.

Cindy spotted a sheet of paper on the counter, and she picked it up. Who could possibly have cleaned her house for her?

A typed note at the bottom of the receipt from the local cleaning service read, *We wanted to make things easier for you. Hurry home. Love, Dad and Mom.*

Cindy caught her lower lip in her teeth and swiped at her eyes with the back of her hand, touched by Ian and Beth's thoughtful gesture. It was hard to leave the life she'd built for herself over the last several years, but it made it easier to know she was moving back to Kentucky, where there were so many people who cared about her.

She glanced at the only window in the apartment,

with its dreary view of a weathered brick wall. Rachel was right. She had always hated that view. Cindy thought of the open vistas of Kentucky, with acres of rolling fields of bluegrass and paddocks full of beautiful horses. She loved looking out her bedroom window at Whitebrook and seeing the paddocks and the barn. The dingy apartment just didn't feel like home anymore.

She headed for the bedroom and began pulling clothes from the closet, piling them on the bed. When she uncovered a box that had been buried in a dark corner, she dragged it out, then sat down on the floor and opened it. A stack of snapshots slid to the floor, and Cindy quickly flipped through them, gazing at pictures of herself with some of the top trainers and jockeys in New York.

She pulled a photo album from the box and opened it to a page of winner's circle photos. There she was on Matt McGrady's chestnut filly, Falcon; another showed her dressed in Whitebrook's blue-and-white silks, on Honor Bright. A picture of her on Wonder's Champion after the Dubai Cup made her think wistfully of the big chestnut stallion and how hard it had been to leave him behind when she left Dubai. In every picture Cindy was astride the proud Thoroughbreds and grinning broadly, with their beaming owners standing at the horses' heads.

She turned page after page, glancing through articles about her wins and the horses she had raced: Dervish in the Riva Ridge Stakes, Gee Whiz in the Gazelle. Cindy could still hear the roar of the crowd echoing faintly in her head. She imagined she could still feel the drumming of hooves on the track, feel the powerful surge of muscles beneath her as she galloped Phoenix to victory in the prestigious Futurity, bringing in a win for Lonnie Gray, one of the top trainers in New York.

She swallowed a lump in her throat, remembering the sense of power as she and the chestnut filly raced past the wire, lengths ahead of the field. Phoenix hadn't wanted to stop running and had fought and danced beneath her. Cindy had to wait until a handler took her head before she jumped to the ground. The owner had been ecstatic, and the people who crowded around the winner's circle kept calling Cindy's name and waving to her.

After she pulled her saddle from the filly's back and checked in with the clerk of the scales, Cindy had pulled off her dirt-spattered goggles. She saw a little blond girl waving eagerly from the rail around the winner's circle, and Cindy tossed the goggles to her. She remembered the expression of pure delight on the child's face when she caught the goggles. It had been an unforgettable day. Cindy smiled at the memory.

She sighed and slapped the album shut. That was all in her past. It seemed so strange not to be looking forward to another race. When she had been a groom and finally started exercise-riding, struggling to earn her jockey's license, all she thought about was racing.

When Whitebrook sold Wonder's Champion to Sheik al-Rihani, Cindy had moved to the United Arab Emirates as his handler, but she was also hoping to race in Dubai while she was there. However, the sheik wouldn't allow her to race. She was a woman; it didn't matter how many races she'd already won. Besides, the sheik believed Cindy had won races not because she was a good jockey, but because she had been lucky enough to ride talented horses such as Champion, horses that would win no matter who was on their backs.

But even with all the frustration and obstacles she had met, racing Thoroughbreds was all Cindy had ever wanted to do. She had refused to give up; no matter what. And now she was being forced to give it all up.

Cindy set the album aside and dug around in the bottom of the box. Wedged in one corner was a slim book she hadn't thought about in years. She pulled it out slowly and turned it over, staring at the diary she had started when she returned from Dubai. She had bought the book at a shop in the airport the day she returned to the United States, a couple of months before her nineteenth birthday. She had started to write in the diary when she began to build her new life in New York.

Her first year in New York had been nearly as difficult as the time she had spent working for the al-Rihanis in Dubai, but in a different way. All her disappointments and setbacks, and finally her successes, had been recorded in this little book.

Cindy shoved the book back into the box. She would have time to read it when she got back to Kentucky, but right then she needed to get things packed. The movers would be at the apartment first thing in the morning, and she had to have everything ready for them. She glanced around the cramped bedroom and nodded firmly. It was time for her to get out of New York.

She started to stuff the photo albums and snapshots back into the box on top of the diary, but she couldn't bring herself to set the diary aside. She pulled it back out of the box and leaned against the side of the bed, staring at the plain cover for several minutes.

Finally she opened it to the first page and began to read.

I'M SITTING IN A MOTEL ROOM NEAR BELMONT PARK, WITH the air conditioner running full blast. Whew! I thought I'd be ready for August in New York after spending eight months in the United Arab Emirates, but it isn't the same at all. New York feels rushed and crowded after living at the al-Rihanis' villa. Still, it feels good to be back in the United States, although it would have been better to come home with Champion instead of leaving him in Dubai. I miss him already. I miss Ben al-Rihani, too, but I am not going to let myself think about him. He and his father can keep their women-aren't-good-enough-to-race attitude in the Arabian desert, where it belongs. I don't have time for it! Tomorrow I'll go the track and see if I can get a job riding for one of the stables. There are races scheduled almost every day this month, so I shouldn't have any trouble getting work. Once I *get settled, I'd better call home and let Dad and Mom know how I'm doing.*

The sun was just brightening the horizon when Cindy got out of the cab and strode up to the back gate at the Belmont Park racetrack. She showed her Kentucky-issued jockey's license to the security guard, who examined it closely before letting her through the gate.

As she walked toward the shed rows, Cindy could hear the familiar noises of the activity around the track's backside. There were no camels bellowing, no hissing of the endless wind sweeping the desert sand, no voices calling out in Arabic. The rattle of wheelbarrows, the whinnies of the horses, and the voices of the trainers and grooms as they worked to prepare the animals for the day all sounded like music to her.

Cindy released a contented sigh. It felt great to be back on familiar turf, even though she had left Champion behind. Her feelings for Ben made her want to go back to Dubai to confront him—she still couldn't believe that someone she had trusted and cared so much about could betray her so easily—but it was too late now to do anything about Ben. And she was sure that even if she returned to Dubai, Sheik al-Rihani wouldn't give her back her job as Champion's handler.

She stepped aside as a groom wheeled a load of soiled bedding past her. She was better off here, anyway, and she knew that Kalim, a young groom at the stable, would take good care of Champion. Ben could take care of himself. She wasn't going to pine away for him!

Cindy strode past exercise riders with riding crops stuffed in the back pockets of their jeans, their helmets in hand. She saw trainers and jockeys talking intently, no doubt reviewing the race schedules for the day and going over last-minute strategies. Cindy longed to be one of the riders deep in conversation with a trainer, working on a plan that would help bring a winner across the finish line. And now that she was here, it wouldn't be long before she was racing again.

Cindy hurried down the aisles, looking for familiar faces, but she didn't see anyone she knew. For a moment loneliness overwhelmed her. She thought about calling home, sure her parents would urge her to return to Kentucky. She'd be safe and secure at Whitebrook again, and able to ride any horse anytime she wanted. Things would be so much easier. The thought of racing Honor Bright on the track once more had her turning toward the track kitchen and the pay phones there. But after a few steps she stopped.

She wasn't going home without giving Belmont her best shot. She was on her own among strangers, but she could handle it. She didn't need the Whitebrook name or a Whitebrook horse to succeed. She was going to prove that she had the talent to be a top jockey on any horse, riding for any farm and any trainer.

Cindy paused near an open stall door. The interior of the stall had been converted to an office, and Cindy stuck her head inside. A heavyset man was hunched over a desk, scribbling on a sheet of paper.

"Excuse me?" Cindy said.

"What?" he snapped without looking up.

"I'm looking for rides," Cindy said, not letting his abruptness intimidate her.

"So are half the kids in New York," the man replied, flipping pages. He continued to ignore Cindy, turning so that his shoulder was to her.

"I have my license," Cindy said, glaring at the back of the man's head.

He finally looked up and gave her a sour look, shaking his head slowly. "How old are you, kid?" he asked.

"Almost nineteen," Cindy said defensively.

"It doesn't matter," he said with a shrug. "I don't hire unknowns. I've got all the jockeys I can use. Try another barn."

Cindy hesitated, tempted to list her credentials for him. Winning the Dubai Cup on Champion was the first thing she would mention, then placing second with Honor Bright in the previous year's Gazelle, but she caught herself before she spoke. Sheik al-Rihani thought she had won the Dubai World Cup because

20

she was riding a great horse. Of course he'd never said it directly, but when he talked about Champion "carrying her to a win," she knew he had meant she was just along for the ride. She'd never know if he was right or wrong unless she proved it, to herself and to everyone else.

I'm not going to use the Whitebrook name to get rides, Cindy thought stubbornly. She would have to earn respect on her own merits.

Cindy turned away from the doorway without another word. If this trainer didn't want her to ride for him, that was his loss, she told herself.

As she continued along the shed row, she passed several horses being prepared for their morning works. A woman wearing a baseball cap with the insignia of a running horse embroidered on the front was watching a groom wrap a bay filly's legs.

"Not quite so tight," she instructed the groom. "We want to support her legs, not cut off the circulation."

"Hi," Cindy said, stopping nearby.

"Can I help you?" the woman said, still concentrating on the clipboard in her hand.

"I'm looking for a job," Cindy said.

The woman looked up at her and narrowed her eyes. "I suppose you want to be a jockey."

"But I am—" Cindy started to say, and then caught herself. She had always thought her life was rough.

Being orphaned at a young age, then living in foster homes until Ian and Beth McLean adopted her, she felt that she had worked hard for, and earned, whatever she had gotten. But living at Whitebrook, where she had been given lots of chances to ride and handle the horses and had learned to race on some of the finest Thoroughbreds in Kentucky, she had taken for granted how she had gotten her start in racing. Now she was getting a taste of how hard it could be to get a chance.

"I'm very good with horses," she said. "I've had a lot of experience in Kentucky."

"I don't have any work right now," the woman said, giving Cindy a friendly smile. "There is no shortage of qualified jockeys around the New York racing circuit. But you might check with Matt McGrady at Stone Ridge Stables. I heard his groom quit yesterday."

Cindy started to protest. Groom? She was a jockey! But instead she nodded politely. "Thanks," she said. "I'll go see him right away."

She left the stable, stopping when she was out of sight to slump against a wall. She wasn't going to be offered any rides right away without throwing Whitebrook's name around. Which meant she was going to have to start at the bottom. Still, this wasn't like Dubai, where even if she had continued to work hard and showed that she deserved a chance, she'd never have gotten to race. If she had to start at the bottom here to prove herself, that's what she would do. She wasn't above shoveling manure and grooming horses, as long as she was eventually given the chance to ride.

Cindy headed purposefully in the direction the trainer had pointed her. When she reached the area where the Stone Ridge stalls were supposed to be, she hesitated. No one was around, but a bay colt had his head outside his stall door. He whinnied and pawed the stall floor impatiently, shoving his nose in Cindy's direction.

"What's the matter with you?" she asked, approaching him cautiously. The colt snorted, and she held her hand out, letting him sniff her palm. When he realized there was nothing in it, he gave another impatient snort, then tossed his head, wheeling around in his stall before thrusting his head outside again.

"You're a little antsy, aren't you?" Cindy said, admiring the colt's elegant head and alert carriage. "You shouldn't get so worked up. You might hurt yourself."

"He should have been on the track half an hour ago."

The deep voice from behind startled Cindy. She quickly stepped away from the stall and spun around. A dark-haired man, not much older than herself, stood near the stalls holding a chestnut filly on a lead.

The man darted Cindy a polite smile. "If you'll

excuse me, I need to get Falcon here into her stall so I can get Moon Shadow ready for his work."

Cindy flipped the latch on an empty stall door and held it open. The stall hadn't been cleaned, and the man grimaced. "I'll take care of your stall as soon as I can, Falcon. I need to get Shadow out to the track."

"Are you Matt McGrady?" Cindy asked.

The trainer nodded as he led the filly into the stall. "Who's asking?" he inquired as he unclipped the lead line.

"I'm looking for a job," Cindy said, latching the stall door after Matt stepped into the aisle. "I heard you were looking for help."

Matt narrowed his eyes and stared hard at her. "I need a groom," he said. "I need someone who can handle horses and will show up every day." He rolled his eyes. "I need someone who isn't afraid to use a pitchfork and knows how to listen to instructions. The last groom I had decided sleeping in was more important than making sure the horses were fed at regular times."

Cindy thought of life at Whitebrook, where the horses always came first. "I'm reliable," she said quickly. "And I've been working with horses my whole life. You won't be sorry if you hire me."

Matt frowned thoughtfully and folded his arms across his chest. "You can give Falcon a flake of hay.

24

Her net is in that tack box, and my office and store-room are in the stall on the other side of Moon Shadow's."

He snapped a lead onto the bay colt's halter and brought the Thoroughbred out of his stall. While he was clipping him to the crossties in the aisle, Cindy grabbed the hay net and walked to an open door, where a few bales of hay and a lidded can of grain sat, along with bags of supplements, bandages, and some pieces of tack. A card table covered with clipboards, papers, and a calculator was shoved against one wall, with a folding chair propped beside it. Cindy filled the net with hay, then returned to Falcon's stall. When she entered the stall, the filly tried to shove her out of the way, grabbing at the feed.

"No," Cindy said firmly, pushing Falcon's nose away. When the filly pinned her ears and tried to grab the hay again, Cindy stood her ground, refusing to let the pushy horse threaten her. Finally Falcon stepped back, waiting until Cindy was out of the stall before she tore into the hay.

Matt was nodding in approval when Cindy turned after closing the stall door. "She doesn't intimidate you," he said.

Cindy shook her head. "She's a little pushy," she said, raising her eyebrows at the trainer. "Do you always let your horses shove you around?"

"The last groom was afraid of Falcon," he said. "Once that filly knows she can get away with something, she doesn't quit."

"And I'll bet she just keeps getting more aggressive, doesn't she?" Cindy asked.

Matt nodded. "But it's the same trait that tells me she's going to be a great racehorse," he said.

Cindy thought of Champion, who had been aggressive and unruly but had run magnificently. She smiled to herself. "It isn't always a bad thing," she agreed. "But she needs to have some manners, too." Champion had a reputation for being strong-minded and difficult, but she had learned to handle the big chestnut stallion, and he had responded well to her.

Cindy glanced back at Falcon, who was happily munching her hay. The chestnut filly was nowhere near the caliber of a Triple Crown winner such as Champion, but Matt was right. Falcon had some obvious good qualities. "Firm, consistent handling," she said out loud, gazing at the filly. "She needs to know her limits without having her arrogance crushed."

"You do know horses," Matt said, sounding impressed.

Instead of replying, Cindy turned her attention to Moon Shadow, a well-built colt with long, solid legs and a deep chest. She grabbed a brush from the bucket in front of his stall and began grooming the colt, running the soft brush lightly down his smooth shoulder and flank.

She glanced up to see Matt watching her, a surprised look on his face.

"I do know how to groom," she said, amused by the trainer's startled expression. "I thought you needed to get him on the track. I'll finish brushing him while you get his tack."

"What's your name?" Matt asked.

"Cindy," she said. "Cindy Blake." She continued to sweep the brush along Moon Shadow's glossy flank. It wasn't dishonest to use her real parents' last name, she reassured herself. And no one would think to associate her with Ian McLean or Whitebrook if she went by the name Blake.

"Is that what you want on your employment papers?" the trainer asked.

"Does that mean I'm hired?" Cindy asked, pulling a hoof pick from the grooming bucket.

"I'll pay fair wages," Matt said.

"Good enough," Cindy replied, pausing to reach up and shake Matt's extended hand. She turned her attention back to Moon Shadow. "Are these the only two horses you have?"

"Right now," Matt said. "If I can do well enough

with my own horses, I'm hoping some of the other owners will let me train for them."

"How long have you had horses at Belmont?" Cindy asked.

"I was working with a trainer in Florida until a few months ago," Matt said. "When I was able to buy a couple of Thoroughbreds, I decided it was time to get out on my own. We may be small now," he added quickly, "but it won't take long to get established." He pointed at the chestnut filly, who was tearing a mouthful of hay from her net. "Falcon is going to be my great success story. She's my ticket to fame and fortune."

Cindy gazed at Falcon. She doubted the filly would ever do anything spectacular, but she kept that thought to herself. Once again she was using Whitebrook's racing stock as a comparison, and once again she realized how lucky she had been to grow up there. Besides, she reminded herself, the filly deserved a chance to prove herself, just as much as Cindy did. "It's good to have dreams," she said.

"I intend to make my dreams real," Matt replied firmly.

"What about Moon Shadow?" Cindy ran her hand along the bay colt's foreleg. "He has good bones, and he's built like a tank. He looks like he'd make a solid distance horse."

Matt frowned at her, a puzzled look on his face.

"You really do know your horses, don't you? Where did you come from?"

"I grew up in Kentucky," Cindy said. "You can't help learning a few things about horses when you live in Thoroughbred country."

Matt nodded. "I guess," he said. "I'll be right back with Shadow's tack." He left without asking any more questions.

Cindy sighed to herself. She had just signed on with a green trainer who probably knew less about conditioning racehorses than she did. This wasn't the best way to get back into racing. But at least she had a job, and she'd be at the track every day. Eventually she would get a chance to race.

Matt returned with Moon Shadow's saddle. "We'll take care of your paperwork after I get done with Shadow," he said, settling the saddle on the colt's back. "My exercise rider is waiting. Meanwhile, you can clean the stalls."

"Sure," Cindy said, unclipping Shadow from the crossties and handing his lead to Matt. When the trainer led the colt toward the track, Cindy grabbed the wheelbarrow handles, but hesitated as she watched Shadow walk away.

She glanced over her shoulder at Falcon. "We're going to get along just fine, aren't we?" she said when the filly swiveled her ears in Cindy's direction. "And when you debut on the track, I'm going to be the one riding you to a win. We'll show them all, won't we, girl?"

Falcon snorted again and turned her attention back to her hay. Cindy rolled the wheelbarrow into Moon Shadow's stall and went to work.

That night when she sat down on her bed in the motel room, she took her new diary off her nightstand and opened it, then rested her back against the wall and began to write.

This is my last night in the motel. Matt told me I can put a cot in the storage room and keep an eye on the horses at night. I can't believe I'm working as a groom for a tiny stable, but Matt is nice, and I like his horses. I called home to let Dad and Mom know how I'm doing. Dad was very happy to hear that I'm back in the United States. He said my room is waiting if I want to come home. I told him about my job here. So what if I'm just a groom, and Stone Ridge is virtually an unknown stable? I have a good feeling about the future.

FOR THE LAST COUPLE OF WEEKS I'VE BEEN SLEEPING IN THE *storage room at Stone Ridge's stabling area. So far the only job I have is grooming Moon Shadow and Falcon. Moon Shadow has already run a couple of races and was in the money, but he hasn't won a race yet. Matt has decided not to race Falcon until next spring. She may not have great bloodlines like the Whitebrook horses, but she is smart and eager to run. I'd like to be the one to ride her in her first race, and win!*

I've seen a few jockeys I recognize, but since I rode most of my races in Kentucky and that was over a year ago, no one seems to remember me. I've been trying to get horses to exercise-ride, but it's really tough without mentioning Whitebrook. It's going to start getting cold, so I really need enough money to get an apartment. It seems almost impossible—everything is so expensive.

Okay, right now I need to put my diary away and get to work!

It was almost ten o'clock on a Friday morning in late September when Cindy walked Moon Shadow back from the wash rack. She needed to get him ready to race that afternoon. Matt was sure the colt was finally going to break his maiden and win his first race. Cindy had thought about asking if she could ride him, but Matt had no idea that she was an experienced rider, let alone a licensed jockey. Cindy knew she had to be patient, but she felt as though she were back in Dubai, watching other people ride while she was stuck on the ground.

As she passed the end of a shed row, Cindy noticed a flashy black colt in one of the wash racks. "He sure is nice-looking," she commented to the dark-haired girl who was crouched near the colt's front legs. The girl finished rinsing the last bit of soap from the horse's fetlocks, then rose. "His name is Texas Turbo," she said, replacing the hose on its rack against the wall. "We just brought him up from Dallas. I was starting to think the trainer would never decide he was ready to race."

"He looks like he'd be fun to ride," Cindy commented.

"I'm really excited about it," the girl said. "And nervous. This is my first race at Belmont." She pointed at Moon Shadow. "Are you riding him?"

32

"No," Cindy said. She glanced at Moon Shadow. "The owner only has two horses. He doesn't need more than one jockey riding for him."

The girl picked up a towel and rubbed Turbo's wet back with it. She glanced over her shoulder at Cindy. "I've had my apprentice license for just a few months," she said. "It's a good thing they allow me a few years to win enough races to lose my bug." The "bug," or asterisk on the race program, indicated a jockey's apprentice status.

"How many races have you won?" Cindy asked.

"One," the girl admitted, grimacing.

"Thirty-nine to go," Cindy said. She felt a twinge of envy that she couldn't even convince anyone to let her exercise their horses, but this inexperienced jockey had been named on a colt that looked as though he could outrun a bullet. *But that was my choice,* Cindy reminded herself firmly. *If I wanted to do it the easy way, I could be riding, too.*

"My name is Rachel Daniels, by the way," the girl said, rubbing her wet hand on her jeans before offering it to Cindy. "Do you live in Elmont?" Rachel asked.

Cindy tilted her head toward the shed row. "For now, I'm living in the Stone Ridge Stables storage room," she said with a laugh. "I work for Matt McGrady."

"Isn't he the cute dark-haired guy?" Rachel asked.

"I never thought about him being cute," Cindy said. "He's my boss, and that's all."

"So you're not dating him or anything?" Rachel looked relieved. "I'd like to meet him."

Cindy thought about how much she had cared about Sheik al-Rihani's son, Ben. It had been Ben who convinced his father to hire Cindy as Champion's handler when they took the stallion to Dubai the previous winter. She had trusted Ben and thought he liked her, making it doubly devastating when he had betrayed her. She could still hear Ben's voice when she overheard him telling his father that a woman's place was in the home, not on the racetrack. And that was after he had promised her over and over that he would try to convince his father to let her race one of his colts. *No*, Cindy thought. *I can get knocked down and trampled by a dozen horses, but bruises and cuts heal. It doesn't seem as though my feelings ever will.*

"Where do you live?" Cindy asked Rachel.

"When one of the other jockeys moved to California I was able to get her apartment," Rachel said. "It's hard to find an affordable place around here."

"It must be nice to have a real bedroom to sleep in," Cindy said wistfully, thinking of her cot and sleeping bag.

Rachel laughed. "For what it costs me in rent, I think I'd probably be better off living at the track." She gave Cindy a thoughtful look. "I've been thinking about getting a roommate to share the rent. Would you be interested?"

Cindy hesitated, mentally calculating how much money she had in her savings account and how much Matt paid her. The thought of having a real bedroom, a private bathroom, and a kitchen to cook her meals was too tempting. "I'd love to," she said. Moon Shadow gave a firm tug on his lead, reminding Cindy that she had a job to do. "But right now I have to get this guy back to the stables."

"I'll come over as soon as I get Turbo put up," Rachel said, unclipping the colt from the crossties. "You can move in tonight."

That afternoon Rachel stood at the viewing paddock, waving to Cindy when she brought Moon Shadow around for his jockey. After handing the colt off to the pony rider, Matt and Cindy joined Rachel at the rail. The other seven horses entered in the race had better times than Moon Shadow, who had been listed as the long shot.

"His odds are almost embarrassing," Matt said, grimacing at the numbers on the electronic tote board.

"He'll do great, I'm sure," Rachel said quickly, smiling up at Matt.

Cindy felt a little left out as Rachel and Matt began

talking, so she focused her attention on the track and Moon Shadow. When the starting bell rang, the jockey had some trouble getting the colt out of the gate. Cindy frowned. She knew she could have gotten him off to a better start. Beside Cindy, Matt groaned loudly as the colt struggled to catch up with the rest of the field.

"He'll pick it up at the end," Cindy said, giving Matt a quick glance. "He just needs to get a feel for the pace." She hoped she was right. Matt was counting on Shadow placing in the money that day.

Cindy held her breath, willing the bay colt to stretch out and get into a distance-eating pace. She wanted to scream at the jockey, who seemed to be holding Shadow back. But in spite of the jockey's interference, Shadow hit his pace, and within a couple of furlongs he had closed the gap, moving up with the leaders.

"Go!" Cindy screamed. On the other side of Matt, Rachel was jumping up and down, yelling for Shadow, while Matt gripped the rail, his eyes riveted on the racing colt.

"He's going to do it!" Cindy cried as Shadow slipped past the horse in third place and started to overtake the number two horse. When the race ended, Matt's three-year-old had finished in a solid second place. Cindy turned to congratulate Matt as Rachel flung her arms around his neck, giving him an excited victory hug. Cindy smiled to herself. Rachel certainly didn't waste any time.

"I'll take care of Shadow," Cindy said, taking the colt's lead when the jockey joined them at the rail.

"I'll meet you and Rachel at the track kitchen," Matt offered. "I'm going to buy all of us a hamburger and french fries for our second-place victory dinner."

Cindy nodded, although she wasn't about to ruin Rachel and Matt's romantic victory dinner by joining them. She knew Rachel wanted to get to know Matt better, and she would rather spend her time with the horses, anyway. She took her time cooling out the colt and waited at the veterinarian's barn for his drug test.

After she bathed and fed Shadow and Falcon, Cindy threw her few belongings in her suitcase. She folded up the camp cot Matt had loaned her, and in minutes her corner of the storage room was empty.

"You missed dinner," Rachel said from the doorway. She grinned at Cindy. "Thanks for giving me a chance to get to know Matt a little better. We had a nice time."

"Cool," Cindy said. "I'm glad you two hit it off. Matt's a great guy."

"Are you ready to leave?" Rachel asked.

Cindy gave the storage room a quick glance to be sure she had everything. "Definitely," she said, grabbing her sleeping bag. "Let's go!"

Rachel's apartment was only a few miles from the track. It was small, with a tiny kitchen–dining room combination and a little living room. The view from the only window was of a dingy brick wall.

"At least it lets in some light," Rachel said when Cindy stared at the dismal scene. "And look," she added, opening a door. "You have your own bedroom!"

"It's perfect," Cindy said, setting her suitcase on the floor. The bedroom was more like a large closet than a real room, but there was space for a bed and a dresser, and Cindy was sure she could make it homey.

The next afternoon Cindy and Rachel explored secondhand stores for furniture that Cindy could afford. They found a bed, complete with a headboard, and a matching dresser. "And I can still afford a lovely light," Cindy said, holding up a little brass table lamp. She rubbed at the tarnished base with her finger. "What luxuries."

That night after she put her clothes into the little chest of drawers, Cindy sat on the edge of her new bed. "I guess I'm home," she said to herself, thinking back to the al-Rihanis' elegant villa. Even the grooms' quarters in the stables were nicer than the apartment she was now sharing with Rachel. She shook her head hard. *I'm not going to think about any of that. Champion is happy and well cared for, and Ben and Dubai are history.*

But when she lay down to sleep that night, her

thoughts kept drifting to the months she had spent in the United Arab Emirates. She couldn't get Champion, or Ben, out of her mind. She wondered if Ben missed her at all, and she hoped the chestnut stallion was all right. In the morning she would write Kalim, Champion's groom, and ask him how the horse was doing.

"Are you going to be ready to leave pretty soon?" Cindy asked Rachel a few mornings later. Rachel was still sitting at the little table in the kitchen, staring into a cup of coffee. Her unbrushed hair was a tangled mess, and her eyes were bleary. Cindy smoothed her hand over her short blond hair and tapped her foot impatiently. She had been ready to leave for an hour, but Rachel seemed to take an eternity to wake up.

"As soon as I can keep my eyes open," Rachel said, yawning hugely. She took another gulp of coffee. "I'm just not a morning person."

Cindy gnawed at the inside of her mouth in frustration. She couldn't really get upset, since Rachel was giving her rides to the track. But Cindy liked to be one of the first people there in the morning and see the first horses go out for their works. She hated to miss a minute of the action around the backside. Besides, the more the trainers saw her there early, the sooner they would recognize how serious she was about racing.

It took only a couple more mornings of showing up

late for her to check out the bus route that ran from the street in front of the apartment to the track.

"Good for you," Rachel said, looking unconcerned when Cindy told her she was going to start riding the bus. "I just don't have your motivation to be there before the crack of dawn."

"Maybe if you got to bed earlier, you'd be able to get up sooner," Cindy suggested.

Rachel shrugged. "I manage," she said. "But I still need to have a social life." She frowned at Cindy. "Maybe you should try going out and having some fun sometime."

"No, thanks," Cindy said. She knew of several jockeys who had been injured on the track, or had caused horses to be injured or killed, because they had been too busy partying to get enough sleep. Taking horses out for the early morning works without a clear head was a dangerous mistake.

Cindy already knew how hard it was to ride with an injury. Her shoulder still bothered her, even though the accident on Honor Bright at Whitebrook had happened nearly three years before. That mishap had taught her a lesson she would never forget. She was going to build a solid reputation as a conscientious jockey, not a careless one.

Cindy arrived at the track before daylight broke, and after she took care of Moon Shadow and Falcon, she headed to Maggie Ward's Clearcrest barn, her riding helmet in hand.

"Do you have any horses that need working?" she asked the trainer, the same way she had every morning. She waited for the usual answer, no, but that morning Maggie gazed hard at Cindy for a moment, as if evaluating her, then nodded.

"I'm short a rider this morning," she said. "I'll give you a try."

"Thank you!" Cindy nearly shouted. *At last!*

The colt Maggie pointed out for Cindy was a tall bay with a white star. "Cashemin," she said, patting the Thoroughbred's shoulder. "He can be a bit of a handful, but he's pretty good once he gets on the rail. I don't think you'll have too much trouble with him."

"We're going to do just fine, aren't we, boy?" Cindy replied, giving the horse's nose a quick rub.

The energetic colt danced at the rail while Maggie helped Cindy into the saddle. She nodded briefly, and Maggie stepped back. Cashemin pulled at the reins as Cindy guided him onto the track, and she felt the strain in her shoulder. But she was riding at last.

Maggie had predicted the colt's behavior exactly. After a couple minutes of testing Cindy's mettle, he settled into long, steady strides. Cindy felt a broad grin stretching her face as she stood in the stirrups, cantering Cashemin along the rail, enjoying the wonderful sense of being where she belonged. When she returned the sweating colt to Maggie, the trainer was giving Cindy a quizzical look.

"You're a natural," she said. "Or else you've done a lot more than exercise a few horses."

Cindy hopped from the colt's back and pulled her helmet off. "He's a very nice horse," she said.

"I have a couple of others for you to ride," Maggie said. "Regularly, if you want."

"Absolutely," Cindy said. At last she was making progress.

A few days later she took another of Maggie's colts, a black called Festival, onto the track for morning works. The energetic colt tossed his head, fighting to move out, but Cindy held him in, keeping him at a prancing trot. There was a steady ache deep in her shoulder as Festival yanked at the reins, but Cindy gritted her teeth. She was finally getting to exercise some spirited horses. She wasn't going to let her shoulder stop her.

Festival gave a little buck, which Cindy sat easily. When the colt realized that he couldn't get rid of her, he settled down and moved to the rail, where he promptly responded to her cues.

As she was coming off the track she saw Lonnie Gray, one of the most well known trainers at Belmont, sending a rider out on a gray colt. The jockey clearly had his hands full, fighting the defiant colt the whole time, trying to get him on the rail and moving. Cindy watched closely, trying to see what the rider might do differently to manage the fiery horse better.

"Keep him busy," she murmured to herself. "You're reacting to him instead of telling him what to do." She shook her head as the colt nearly got away from the frustrated rider. "I know I could handle that colt better than that," she said firmly, taking Festival to where Maggie was waiting for him.

That afternoon as she was getting ready to leave the track, Matt stopped her. "I saw you riding that colt of Maggie Ward's today," he said. "I didn't know you could ride like that."

Cindy wrinkled her nose at him. "Now you know," she said smartly.

"Do you want to start working Moon Shadow for me?" he asked. "Rachel is going to start working Falcon."

"Sure," Cindy said. Ever since the day she had introduced Matt and Rachel, they had spent a lot of time together. Cindy was glad they liked each other, but it made her think of Ben, and she wished things had turned out differently for them. But there was nothing she could do to change that now. She had to focus on her career.

After she had finished exercising Moon Shadow

one morning, Cindy walked the colt along the back-side to cool him out. As she strolled past the small stalls facing away from the track, she was surprised to catch a movement in the dark interior of one stall. This late in the year, the back stalls were rarely used. They usually held the overflow of horses during the track's busy season, and most of the horses that were kept there were only at the track for a day or so.

Cindy led Shadow toward the stall, slowing when a horse shoved its nose out of the door and nickered softly.

"What are you doing stuck back here?" Cindy asked, admiring the filly's finely chiseled head. The chestnut filly had a bright, alert look, in spite of being in such an isolated location. She bobbed her nose in Cindy's direction and whinnied loudly, drawing Cindy closer.

Cindy rubbed the filly's red-gold poll, smoothing the auburn forelock over a narrow blaze that streaked down the horse's face. The filly reminded her a little of Ashleigh's Wonder, the orphaned foal Ashleigh Griffen had raised to become a Derby-winning mare and the dam of many great horses for Whitebrook, including Champion.

"Who are you?" Cindy asked out loud. She peered into the stall, glad to see that the interior had fresh bedding and water. At least the filly wasn't being neglected. The chestnut filly nudged at Cindy's hand, demanding attention. "You must be kind of lonely back here," Cindy said, petting her.

Behind Cindy, Shadow stamped impatiently. "I'll be back," she told the filly. "I want to know your story." She quickly finishing cooling the bay colt and bathed him thoroughly. She ran her hands down his legs to feel for any heat or tenderness, then wrapped each one carefully. "You and I are going to set some distance records," she said, settling his blanket on his tall back. Shadow grunted softly, as if agreeing with her. "Once Matt lets me race you, that is."

After filling Shadow's hay net and checking Falcon's water, Cindy headed for the track office.

"I'd like to know who the trainer is for a filly located in one of the back barns," Cindy said, giving the woman at the office the filly's stall number.

"Lonnie Gray is the man you need to see," the woman said. "You can find him at the GeeGee Stables."

"Thanks," Cindy said. Even though it was none of her business, she couldn't get the filly off her mind.

GeeGee Stables took up most of one shed row. Cindy hurried past stalls holding obviously well-bred racehorses, looking for the office.

"That filly is a waste of feed," Lonnie Gray said flatly when Cindy found him in his office. "Gloria

Goldrich sent her here from the breeding farm to see if she was sound enough to race. She isn't. She never will be." The tall, thin trainer leaned back in his chair. He propped his feet next to a state-of-the-art computer on his desk and gazed at Cindy. "She went lame the first time I had her on the track. With so many other horses around, I doubt Mrs. Goldrich even remembers she's here. I guess that chestnut will be going to auction next month. We're heading for Florida, and I don't want to drag her along."

"What kind of injury does she have?" Cindy asked.

"She was born with weak tendons," Lonnie said. "She bowed one the first time she did anything more strenuous than walk. I have horses here worth hundreds of thousands of dollars. Why would I waste my time on a horse that won't ever set a hoof on the track for a race?" He dropped his feet to the ground and leaned forward. "I suppose the tendon could heal and strengthen with time and therapy, but I don't have it to put into her. She isn't worth it. We have too many sound horses to waste the energy."

Cindy took a deep breath. "I'd like to spend some time working with her, if it's okay with you."

"I'm not going to pay anyone to try rehabilitating her," Lonnie said, shaking his head.

"I don't expect you to pay me," Cindy replied. "I think there's something special about her." She knew she wasn't being logical, but she could relate to the filly's situation. If there was something she could do to help the chestnut get a fair shot on the track, she needed to do it.

"Aren't you an exercise rider?" Lonnie asked, looking intently at Cindy.

She nodded. "I'm working for Matt McGrady and Maggie Ward," she said.

Lonnie sighed. "You'd be wasting your time working with that crippled filly," he told her. "If you're that bored, I could give you stalls to clean. Maybe even find a sound horse for you to exercise, if you want to handle a horse that badly."

Cindy inhaled sharply. Exercise-ride for Lonnie Gray? That would be perfect. But she thought of the filly, bright-eyed and lonely, and she shook her head. "I want to work with the filly," she said, wondering where her common sense had gone.

"I think it's a bad idea," Lonnie said. "What do you know about leg injuries?"

"I'm experienced with horses," Cindy said, feeling desperate. "I spent a lot of time at a breeding and training farm in Kentucky. I know I could help her."

"So you know a little bit about horses," he said, then shrugged indifferently. "It's your time you'd be wasting," the trainer went on, rolling his eyes. "Just don't expect anything great, and as far as I'm concerned, she's still going to auction before I leave next month."

"Okay," Cindy said. Maybe it would be a waste of her time, but the filly deserved a second chance. If she could get her sound before Lonnie left for Florida, maybe he wouldn't get rid of her. Cindy hurried off in search of the track vet to get more information on the filly's condition.

"She was exercised too hard too soon, that's all," the vet said when Cindy described the filly. "She could come back with the right therapy and patience." He detailed an exercise plan and explained how Cindy should soak and wrap the filly's leg to speed the healing and strengthen her tendons.

"You're my new project," she informed the chestnut when she returned to her stall. Cindy put the filly on the mechanical walker, admiring the horse's long strides and smooth action. Even if she couldn't do a lot of racing, she had traits that she could pass on to her offspring.

Cindy realized she had been so focused on getting permission to work with the horse, she had forgotten to ask Lonnie the filly's name. She hurried back to Lonnie's office.

"Her name is Phoenix," he said in response to Cindy's question.

"Like the myth about the bird rising from the

ashes," Cindy said, remembering the story from her sophomore English class. "It suits her perfectly." She went by the library on her way home and picked up some veterinary textbooks and training manuals.

"What are you studying?" Rachel asked when Cindy walked into the apartment, her arms loaded with books.

Cindy quickly explained about Phoenix.

"Lonnie Gray has a reputation for throwing away horses that don't meet his expectations," Rachel said. "He only works with the best."

"That's fine," Cindy said. "I'm going to show him that if he doesn't give this filly a fair chance, he's overlooking one of the best horses at the track."

She sat up late reading, then finally set the books aside and picked up a pen and her diary.

Phoenix and I are going to prove we deserve better. She's got the spark and the conformation to run well, and I've got the know-how and the patience to bring her back. I'm not going to let her go to auction. She deserves a better fate than being bought for dog food. And I know it sounds like a long shot, but maybe one day I'll ride her in a race and we'll win!

4

IF I CAN GET LONNIE TO SEE PHOENIX'S TRUE POTENTIAL, MAYBE he won't advise her owner to send her to auction before he leaves for Florida. But time is running out, and he's always too busy to look at her. I keep thinking about how good I had it in Kentucky. It's tempting to give up and go home, but I don't want to go back until I get to race once or twice here. Who knows when that will be? At this rate I may never get home!

During the quiet winter months, there was little to do at the track except clean stalls and groom horses. Whenever the weather was clear, Cindy took Phoenix out. "Attagirl," she called, jogging the filly on a longe line in the empty area behind the shed rows. She watched closely as Phoenix moved into a canter, trying to see if she was favoring her weak leg at all. As far as Cindy could tell, Phoenix was fine. If she could just get

Lonnie to watch the filly in action, she was sure he would agree with her.

She spent the afternoon soaking Phoenix's leg, trying to figure out how to convince the trainer to let her take the filly onto the track before he left for Florida. Lonnie seemed to have no interest at all in Phoenix. Cindy leaned against the door of Phoenix's stall and sighed.

"I'm afraid Lonnie just agreed to let me work with you so he wouldn't have to worry about you," she said. Phoenix nudged Cindy's shoulder, twitching her lips along the collar of Cindy's jacket. Cindy rubbed the filly's forehead, her own brow wrinkled into a frown. How was she going to get Lonnie to see how well Phoenix was doing when he wouldn't even give her so much as a glance?

"Matt's coming over for dinner," Rachel announced when Cindy got home one evening. "We're going to watch some race tapes so he can give me some pointers." She smiled happily. "And I'm going to impress him with what a fantastic cook I am."

"That's great," Cindy said. It was nice of Matt to offer to help Rachel with her riding. She thought about telling Matt about her own license. If he knew Cindy was licensed, he might let her race Moon Shadow. She was certain she could get the colt to run even better than he'd been running. But Matt still wasn't aware Cindy was anything more than a talented exercise rider who wanted to be a jockey one day. If Cindy didn't start getting more offers to ride, though, she might be forced to tell people about her background at Whitebrook. She certainly wasn't making much progress on her own.

When Matt showed up for dinner, Rachel set the little kitchen table for three, but throughout the meal Cindy felt as though she weren't even in the room. Rachel kept gazing into Matt's eyes, and every time Matt tried to say something to Cindy, Rachel would quickly get his attention back.

Rachel left Cindy alone to wash the dishes while she and Matt went into the living room, and over the sound of the water running, Cindy could hear them talking. She had to remind herself that Rachel wasn't trying to be rude. If Ben had come to dinner, she would have acted the same way.

Cindy sighed at the thought. She still missed Ben, even though he had hurt her feelings. But he was thousands of miles away, and she doubted she would ever see him again.

By the time she went into the living room, Rachel was curled up beside Matt on the sofa, watching a race video. Cindy considered going to her room to leave Matt and Rachel in private, but when she saw the next race start, she hesitated. Analyzing races was a great way to learn. It had always been one of her favorite parts of the morning meetings the stewards held for apprentice jockeys.

She settled on the threadbare recliner that was their only chair, and focused her attention on the television.

"Right there," Matt said, pointing at the screen. "Do you see what the rider on the number four horse is doing, Rachel?"

"Of course I do," Rachel said. "He's bringing the colt ahead of the number seven horse and squeezing through that little gap between number one and number six. That's pretty obvious."

"But that isn't all," Cindy exclaimed, amazed that Rachel hadn't seen the subtle things the jockey did. "He checked the horse just enough so that the number seven horse wasn't feeling pushed, then he brought his crop just past his colt's line of vision so that the horse put on a burst of speed right as the opening widened enough to slip into it. He caught everyone by surprise."

"Exactly!" Matt said, grinning at Cindy. "It's those little details that are going to help you win more races than you lose." He gave Cindy a long questioning look. "Do you spend a lot of time analyzing race tapes?"

Cindy nodded. "I've spent a lot of time—"

"I saw all that, too," Rachel said, interrupting Cindy. "I didn't know you wanted a detailed report, Matt."

Cindy sank back in her chair and exhaled. She had almost told Matt she had spent a lot of time racing and had learned from Ashleigh Griffen, one of the best jockeys in the business. Good thing Rachel never let Matt's attention stray very far from herself.

Rachel jumped from the sofa and shut off the video. "Let's go out," she said to Matt. "We've worked enough today."

"Sure," Matt said agreeably, flashing Cindy an apologetic grin. "Do you want to go with us?"

"I'm sure she doesn't," Rachel answered for Cindy. "Cindy never goes out."

"I have things to do here," Cindy said, nodding. Rachel was right. She never did go out, mostly because she hadn't met anyone around the track who she wanted to date. She found herself comparing everyone to Ben. She couldn't help but feel that when she had left Dubai, she had left a piece of her heart there. "Enjoy yourselves," she said, smiling brightly. But when Matt and Rachel left the apartment, her smile quickly faded.

Cindy sat in the living room for several minutes after they left, feeling lonely and a little sorry for herself. "Maybe I should go back to Kentucky," she said to the empty apartment. "It would be a lot easier than staying here." But if she left, she'd be letting Phoenix down—and giving up her chance to succeed on her own. She went to bed early, reminding herself that spending her evenings home alone wasn't the worst thing she could be doing. She could still be in Dubai, struggling against all odds to prove herself worthy to the sheik and his son.

Instead of feeling sorry for herself, she focused on the problem of how to demonstrate to Lonnie the progress Phoenix was making. But there was no chance he was going to take time away from the horses he was sending down to Florida. She went to bed still trying to figure out a way to solve the dilemma. As she drifted off to sleep, it dawned on her: If she couldn't get Lonnie to go to Phoenix, she'd just have to bring the filly to him.

The next morning she led Phoenix out of her stall and groomed her to perfection. Then she wrapped her front legs to support the tendons. She stepped back to look the filly over. "You look perfect," she said, admiring Phoenix's sleek lines and alert, elegant head. "Lonnie would have to be blind not to see what a great horse you are."

Phoenix tossed her head and stomped impatiently, and Cindy nodded. "You're right," she said. "Let's go show you off." She took a deep breath, then boldly led Phoenix through the shed rows to the GeeGee Stables. Lonnie was coming out of his office as she brought Phoenix down the aisle.

"Is that the lame filly?" he asked, sounding irritated. "I don't have time for her right now."

"I want to take Phoenix onto the track," Cindy said, then waited tensely. She was taking a risk by being so pushy, but this was Phoenix's only chance. Lonnie was leaving the next week. Since he hadn't said anything different, as far as Cindy knew, he still planned to advise Phoenix's owner to send the filly to auction.

"She can't possibly be sound enough to ride," Lonnie said, shaking his head.

"Please let me show you what she can do," Cindy said. "It won't take long, I promise."

Lonnie looked from Cindy to the filly, then shrugged. "I'll be trackside getting some times on a couple of horses," he said. "You can tack her up and bring her over."

Cindy waited until he walked away before she turned to Phoenix, feeling weak with relief. "This is your chance," she murmured to the filly, who flicked her ears and nuzzled Cindy.

Cindy quickly got Phoenix ready to go onto the track, checking and rechecking the leg wraps, making sure the saddle was settled perfectly on the filly's back.

Then she straightened and gnawed nervously at her lower lip, looking Phoenix in the eye. "You have to do better than great," she said, taking the filly's lead line. If Phoenix didn't impress Lonnie right away, there wasn't anything else Cindy could do to help the filly.

When she reached the track, Lonnie was standing by the rail, holding a stopwatch. Cindy watched one of the GeeGee horses thunder along the inside rail, and she felt her heart tighten. That was where she wanted to be, on a well-conditioned, top-bred race-horse, flying along the rail. Instead she was standing trackside with a filly that the trainer had no interest in at all. She turned to Phoenix and patted the filly's glistening neck. "We'll get there," she said softly. "Both of us."

Lonnie turned away from the track and eyed Phoenix for a moment. Cindy was afraid he was going to change his mind about letting her take the filly onto the track. But he walked over to offer her a leg up. "Just jog her a little," he said. "I don't want to see her break down completely out there."

Cindy ground her teeth and guided the filly onto the track. "You're not going to break down," she muttered to Phoenix, moving the filly along the outside rail. Phoenix settled into an easy jog, and Cindy sighed with relief as they circled the track without any problems. All the strength-building exercises they had been doing were paying off. "You're doing great," she told Phoenix, rubbing the filly's sleek neck with her knuckles. She could feel the power in Phoenix's strides, and she wished with all her heart that she could be taking the horse for a prerace warm-up, not just trying to save the filly from an uncertain future. But she rode Phoenix as though they were preparing for the most important race of both their lives.

"Pick up the speed," Lonnie called as they trotted past him.

As Cindy cued the filly into a canter, Phoenix leaned into the bit, trying to shift into racing speed. Cindy fought to hold her down to a slower pace, excited that the filly had the desire to run, worried that she would strain her leg again before she was ready for the stress of a race. Phoenix jerked her head impatiently, giving a hard pull on Cindy's shoulder. Cindy clenched her jaw, ignoring the pain that shot down her arm. She couldn't quit now, not with Lonnie watching.

After several lengths she brought the filly to a stop. Phoenix pranced along the rail, tugging at the bit and fighting to keep going. "Not so fast," Cindy murmured, feeling a little shaky from the deep ache that radiated from her shoulder. She sighed with relief when they reached Lonnie, but the trainer was staring at them, unsmiling. Cindy felt sick, sure Lonnie was going to tell her Phoenix was done for good. She stopped the filly in front of him and braced herself for the bad news.

"I'm impressed," he said blandly. "I never thought she'd come as far as she has. She still seems to be favoring that leg, but it looks like she's doing it more out of habit than because of any injury."

Cindy stared down at him. "What does that mean?" she asked, clutching the reins in her fists.

"Why don't you move her up to the main barn while I'm working with the horses in Florida?" he said. "I'll give you a list of training rations for her, and you can start riding her regularly."

Cindy forgot her sore shoulder. She wanted to leap from Phoenix's back and throw her arms around Lonnie's neck, but instead she nodded calmly. "Great," she said. "I'll do everything I can to bring her around before you get back."

"It's your time," Lonnie said. "If she doesn't pull through by spring, she's still out of here. But it can't hurt to let you try. You handle a racehorse pretty well," he added. "Maybe when I come back I'll have a horse or two for you to exercise."

Cindy hopped from the filly's back. "Thanks," she said, reining in her own elation. Things were looking up for her, and for Phoenix.

• • •

"Are you staying here over Christmas?" Rachel asked Cindy one evening in mid-December.

Cindy nodded. She didn't want to go home without some great success stories to share with her family. So far she couldn't even claim to have ridden a single race at Belmont since her return. "I'm earning a little extra money cleaning stalls for a couple of grooms who won't be here," she told Rachel. "Why?"

"Matt is going to Texas with me to meet my parents," Rachel said happily. "But he'll need someone to take care of the horses while he's gone."

"Of course I'll take care of them," Cindy said. "You two must be getting pretty serious if Matt's going home with you."

Rachel's eyes sparkled. "Very serious," she said, smiling brightly.

It was quiet around the track during the holidays. Cindy spent her time taking care of the horses and trying not to feel sorry for herself. The cold, damp weather made her shoulder ache more than ever, and the dark, quiet apartment made her feel listless and sad.

She phoned home on Christmas morning, forcing herself to sound upbeat when Ian answered the phone.

"Merry Christmas!" she exclaimed. She could hear talk and laughter in the background. It sounded as though everyone at Whitebrook was gathered at the McLeans' cottage. She sank onto the sofa and pulled her sweater tight around her, but she knew the cold, empty feeling that filled her was on the inside, and not because the apartment was chilly.

"Samantha and Tor are here," Ian said after Cindy told him about working with Phoenix. "Sammy has some news to share with you."

"Cindy!"

The sound of her sister's voice brought a smile to Cindy's face. Samantha sounded so happy.

"What's your big news?" Cindy asked, expecting to hear about a new jumper Samantha and Tor had bought.

"Tor and I are moving to Ireland!" Samantha exclaimed. "We'll be working with a top cross-country trainer in County Sligo. Isn't that exciting?"

"Ireland?" Cindy felt her jaw drop. Now she wished she had gone home for Christmas. If Sammy and Tor were moving out of the country, she didn't know when she would ever see them again.

"Yes," Samantha said, chatting on about the exciting new position she and Tor were taking and what a great opportunity it was for them.

"I'm really happy for you," Cindy said. She remembered how excited she had been about going to Dubai, and how badly things had turned out. But Tor

61

and Samantha were going to an English-speaking country, and no matter what else happened, they would have each other. That was more than she'd had.

When Cindy finally got off the phone, the apartment felt too quiet and lonely. She grabbed an apple from the bowl of fruit on the kitchen table and pulled on her jacket, heading out the door.

When she arrived at Belmont, the track seemed lifeless. But there were always stalls to clean. She got her wheelbarrow and manure fork and set to work changing the bedding in Falcon's and Shadow's stalls. Her breath turned to fog in the cold air, and she felt the nip of the icy wind on her cheeks. She had left the apartment without her gloves, and she stopped frequently to warm her hands in her pockets, looking out across the bleak gray skyline. The weather was always beautiful in Dubai. Ben definitely wasn't wearing wool gloves and a scarf to keep warm.

"Forget all that," she snapped at herself. "You can't undo what happened. Get over it."

She put the wheelbarrow away, picked up a bucket of grooming tools, and headed for Phoenix's stall. At the sound of her approach, Phoenix stuck her head into the aisle and whinnied loudly. Cindy went into the stall, smiling a little as the filly eagerly took the apple Cindy had brought her.

"It looks as if we get to spend Christmas together,"

Cindy said, pulling Phoenix's blanket off and hanging it over the stall door. She pressed a rubber currycomb to the filly's shoulder and began grooming her. Phoenix rubbed her forehead against Cindy's shoulder, and Cindy sighed, blinking back a few tears. "At least I have you," she said. "For now, anyway."

I wish spring would get here. I'm tired of not being able to do anything on the track in this rotten weather. I'd like to do more with Phoenix than walk her around the backside. Matt and Rachel should be back from Texas in a couple of days. Nothing is going the way I had hoped it would when I came here last fall, but all I can do is keep trying. I'm not ready to give up yet.

5

Ever since Matt and Rachel came back from Texas, Rachel hasn't been very interested in racing. She stays out so late that she can barely get up in the mornings. I heard one of the other exercise riders complaining to his trainer that Rachel almost caused a bad accident last week. It would be awful if she did get in an accident because she was too tired to pay attention. If I say anything, all she does is get mad at me. She thinks I'm too serious. I don't know, maybe she's right.

"You're going to be late for morning works again," Cindy told Rachel one morning in early February. Her roommate was standing in her bedroom doorway, still in her pajamas, while Cindy was at the apartment door, ready to leave for the track.

"It isn't the end of the world, you know," Rachel said, dragging her hair back from her face.

"The trainers remember which riders are there early and ready to work," Cindy reminded her.

"I'm not worried about getting horses to ride," Rachel said. "Matt told me he's bringing in two new horses, and I know he'll let me work with them."

For a moment Cindy was hurt. Matt hadn't mentioned any new horses to her. But then again, it would make sense that Rachel would know everything Matt was doing. She spent every free minute she had with him.

If things had worked out differently between Cindy and Ben, she would probably be going out every once in a while, too. She certainly wouldn't be spending all her time working with Phoenix or sitting home alone. She wondered if Ben was spending his evenings alone or if he was out enjoying himself. *What does it matter?* she reminded herself irritably.

"It isn't just having horses to work," Cindy snapped at Rachel. "You need to be wide awake to ride a horse on the track. It's too risky to go out there without a clear head." Every jockey had at least one horror story of an accident on the track. Horses and riders were injured every day, or even killed.

"You just worry about you, and I'll worry about me," Rachel insisted stubbornly.

When Cindy got to Belmont, she headed for Stone Ridge to talk to Matt about Falcon. She slowed when she saw

Matt holding a black colt, running his hand along the horse's shoulder. "What do you think of Current Event?" Matt asked her when she walked up to him. "I finally talked a couple of owners into letting me train for them. He's a good-looking three-year-old, isn't he?"

Cindy nodded, glancing up as a gray colt shoved his head out of his stall, his ears pinned flat against his head. "Who is that?" she asked, eyeing the fierce-looking colt.

"Glitz," Matt said. "The van company brought him in from Florida late last night. The driver had some horror stories to tell about that monster. He had to be shipped alone because he attacks the other horses."

"What are you going to do with him?" Cindy asked.

Matt looked discouraged. "I may just have to tell the owner I can't handle him," he said. "But he's got some great breeze times, and I hate to give up before I even get started with him."

"He's good-looking," Cindy said, looking the colt over. Glitz was tall and lean, with the look of a greyhound. The gray colt kept tossing his head and snorting loudly, rolling his eyes at every noise he heard. Cindy shook her head.

"It'll be a few days before they're ready to go on the track," Matt said. "I hope all Glitz needs is a little time to settle in."

"They both look like they're going to be real handfuls out there," Cindy observed, watching Glitz fling his head up and jump sideways in his stall, kicking the wall with both back hooves.

Matt winced at the sound of shod hooves hitting wood. "My plan was for you to keep working with Moon Shadow and Falcon, and I'll have Rachel start riding these two. But now I'm not so sure."

"I'll take him onto the track for you," Cindy said.

Matt stared at her. "Are you sure?" he said.

Cindy nodded. "I know I can handle him," she said confidently. If she could get a terror like Glitz under control on the track, a lot of trainers would have to take notice of her, and she'd be certain of getting offers to ride.

After she had done her work at Matt's barn, Cindy headed for GeeGee Stables. She was surprised to see Lonnie standing in the aisle.

"You came back early," she said.

He nodded. "I had to bring a couple of horses back to the farm," he said. "I thought I would see how things are going here."

"Phoenix is doing great," Cindy said, pointing toward the filly's stall.

Lonnie nodded. "She looks fit," he remarked. "Maybe you should take her onto the track and let me see her run."

"Sure! I'll get her out right away."

Lonnie walked away, and Cindy quickly got Phoenix out, clipping her to the crossties. When she took the filly to the track, she found Lonnie talking with another trainer. Without saying a word to her, he indicated with a bob of his head that she should take the filly onto the track.

"He isn't even paying attention," Cindy grumbled, riding Phoenix through the gap at the rail. The filly pranced as Cindy adjusted her grip on the reins, settling herself in the saddle. "You feel ready to go today," she told the excited horse.

It took all the strength she had to keep Phoenix down to a trot. Her arm ached with the strain, and before they had gone half a circuit, Phoenix's shiny coat was streaked with sweat. Cindy eyed the lather on the filly's shoulder and grimaced. "Relax a little," she murmured, then almost laughed. Phoenix wasn't the only one who was on edge that morning. Cindy took a deep breath and exhaled, trying to loosen the grip she had on the reins. She moved her hands, looking at the dark marks her damp palms had left on the leather.

"We're both getting worked up over Lonnie being here, and he isn't even watching us," she said to Phoenix.

Once Cindy got her own attention back on working, Phoenix eased up, and they completed the warm-up jog at an easy pace. Cindy debated whether or not she should move the filly up a gear, but when she saw Lonnie standing at the rail, he gestured to her to come off the track.

She sighed. She and Phoenix hadn't given the best performance just then, and she hoped he wasn't going to use that to make a decision about Phoenix's future.

"She's got a lot of energy, doesn't she?" she asked, wanting Lonnie to notice the filly's strengths. "She can really move out."

"That isn't my concern with her," Lonnie replied, holding the filly's headstall while Cindy hopped to the ground. "It's how sound she is, and if she can hold up to the stress of a race." He ran his hands along Phoenix's legs and around her shoulder, looked at her gums and into her eyes, then turned to Cindy. "I have to admit you've done a good job with her," he said. "I still don't know if she can handle a race, but I'll give you until the start of the spring meet."

Two days later Matt met her at the rail with Glitz tacked and ready to go onto the track. The colt fought Matt, stopping to rear and strike at the air with his hooves, biting at the trainer, and dancing around. Cindy could tell it took everything Matt had to keep the colt in hand.

Nervous excitement buzzed through her at the thought of taking the powerful colt onto the track. Riding Glitz was either going to end her career or bump it into a higher gear.

Cindy vaulted onto the colt's back and put her feet in the stirrups, making sure she was settled deep into the saddle before giving Matt a brief nod. The trainer released the colt onto the track, and Cindy braced herself, ready for anything.

"No flying lessons, do you understand?" she told the colt, who danced along the rail, trying to pull the reins from her hands. Glitz jerked his head, wrenching her shoulder, and Cindy gritted her teeth, determined not to let the colt get the better of her. But even though he was wired, the colt did nothing worse than lean heavily on her hands and try to gallop faster and faster. Cindy smiled grimly. If her shoulder could take the punishment, she and Glitz might just have a fighting chance. But as soon as she got him going along the rail, the colt suddenly hit the brakes, sending her flying over his shoulder. She hit the ground with a thud, feeling the landing in her bad shoulder.

She jumped to her feet, the reins still in her hand. "Nice trick," she told the colt, who stared at her wide-eyed.

"Do you want to quit?" Matt asked from the rail. "You don't have to ride him, Cindy."

Cindy eyed Glitz for a moment, then turned to Matt. "Just give me a leg up," she said, ignoring his question.

By the time they had gone around the track a few times, Glitz was breathing hard and soaked with sweat, and Cindy was sure she must have dislocated her shoulder. It throbbed so badly, she was afraid she was going to be sick from the pain. But she couldn't tell Matt her shoulder was bothering her. Instead she forced herself to smile at him as she handed the exhausted colt over.

"That was some riding," he said, taking the lead.

"He's a real bullet," Cindy exclaimed. "I could feel it in him. He'll burn up the track in a race."

"The trouble is, I don't think he's ever finished a race," Matt said. "I heard from some people in Florida that he throws a fit when he gets on the track with other horses."

"Let me keep working with him," Cindy said. "If we're consistent with him, maybe he'll get over it. He's powerful, Matt. You have to give him a chance to run."

"It's your choice," Matt told her.

"Fine," Cindy said. "When can I ride him again?"

A grin tugged at the corners of Matt's mouth. "You're pretty stubborn, aren't you?"

"You'd better believe it," Cindy said, nodding firmly.

"The day after tomorrow," Matt said. As he walked away with the colt, she reached up to clutch her arm, and hurried to the jockeys' lounge, where she sat in the locker room with an ice bag on her shoulder until the cold numbed the pain. What she really needed was rest. But if riding a difficult horse meant more trainers would notice her, she'd be getting more and more rides as soon as the spring meet started up—that is, if her shoulder held up.

For the next couple of weeks Cindy rode both Glitz and Current Event. The first time Rachel watched her take Glitz onto the track, she stood at the rail, a sullen look on her face. Cindy knew the other jockey had been excited about working with the new horses. Glitz went into a bucking fit when Cindy insisted on keeping him down to a slow canter, and Cindy felt every jolt in her shoulder, finally losing her grip on the reins and sailing over the gray colt's head. She got back on, and Glitz proceeded to fight her every step of the way. When she finished working Glitz, Rachel was looking relieved.

"I'm glad it wasn't me on that colt," she said, holding his head while Cindy swept dirt off her clothes.

Cindy lost track of the number of times Glitz threw her, but she still felt she was making progress with the unruly horse, so she tried to remain encouraged. She didn't tell Matt about her troublesome shoulder for fear that he wouldn't let her ride for him anymore.

Her only rest came when she worked with Phoenix. "It's too bad there isn't a swimming pool here for us," she told the filly, holding her while she doused Phoenix's legs with a hose. "I'd get in there with you and soak my shoulder."

Cindy had been right about working with Glitz, however. The more time she spent on the track with the difficult colt, the more attention she got from the other trainers at Belmont. Cindy eagerly accepted every chance to ride, but the increasingly difficult horses she worked with meant a lot of spills. And every time she came off another horse, she knew she was doing even more damage to her bad shoulder. But she couldn't quit. Not now.

"Glitz is more wired today than usual," Matt told Cindy one morning, holding the gray colt's head while Cindy adjusted her helmet. "Keep a tight rein on him."

"I'll do my best," Cindy said, vaulting onto Glitz's saddle. She could feel the tense energy that hummed in the colt's muscles, and she grimaced. She felt as though she had just climbed onto a rocket that was ready for launch.

As soon as they got on the track, she headed the excited horse clockwise, Matt's warm-up instructions running through her mind. But the colt felt like a wreck just waiting to happen. Glitz needed to be worn down, not warmed up!

After a few miles of steady jogging, the colt's coat

was only slightly damp with sweat, and Cindy moved him off the rail, pushing him to a gallop. Glitz fought her grip, and Cindy's shoulder, sore from being tugged and wrenched repeatedly for the last few weeks, ached deep within the joint. If she kept this up, by the time the season started in March, she would be too crippled to ride. All the horses she had been exercising would go to other jockeys. What good would that do her?

But Cindy gritted her teeth and forced the colt to stay his course. When they finished the workout, she hurried to the jockeys' lounge. She dug some aspirin from her locker, downing the tablets with a swallow of coffee, hoping the hot drink would dissolve the pain pills faster.

Then she took a long shower, letting the hot water run over her shoulder for what seemed like hours. Finally the ache faded a little, and Cindy dressed, leaving the locker room and heading for home.

She sank back on her bed that night, exhausted, but her mind was whirring with worry. She couldn't sleep. Finally she turned on her bedside lamp and pulled her diary out of her nightstand.

The spring meet starts in less than a month. I know Phoenix will be ready to race by then. Her leg is in great shape, and Lonnie even sounds a little excited about putting her on the track. Matt told me I can race Glitz. I don't know how I feel about that. This could be the start of my new, self-made career as a jockey. But my shoulder is giving me so much trouble. If I keep going the way I have been, I'll be too crippled to ride any of the horses!

6

Phoenix looks fantastic. Maybe after he sees her work today, Lonnie will find a race for her. I'm excited about getting a chance to show him how I handle a horse in a race, and prove to him that Phoenix is worth saving, but I'm a little nervous, too. It will be the first time I've raced since I rode Honor in the Gazelle almost a year and a half ago. My shoulder is bothering me a lot, but I can't say anything, or I'll never get a chance to ride. Nobody is going to want a jockey who isn't healthy.

When Cindy got to the track in the morning, she went straight to Phoenix's stall. "Time to get to work," she said to the filly, who tossed her head and nickered in greeting. Cindy clipped a lead line to Phoenix's halter and brought her into the aisle. "I hope Lonnie has a few minutes today," Cindy said, picking up a hoof pick. "He needs to see you in action."

Lonnie walked by as Cindy was bandaging Phoenix's front legs. "That looks perfect," he said, leaning down to feel the wrap on the filly's weak leg. "I couldn't have done it better myself." He stepped back and narrowed his eyes, gazing at the filly. "Let's breeze her," he said.

Cindy felt her jaw go slack. "Breeze her?" she repeated. "Right now?"

Lonnie nodded. "If you want to race her, we're going to need to get a time for the records. What, are you having second thoughts?"

"No," Cindy said quickly. "Phoenix is sound, and I still want to race her."

"Fine. Let's get over to the track and see what she can do," Lonnie said.

"I'd like to warm her up on the longe line before we take her out," Cindy said.

Lonnie gave an indifferent shrug. "Let me know when you're ready to tack her up," he said. "I'll be in my office."

Cindy watched him walk away, then turned to Phoenix and patted her sleek shoulder. "At least he's giving you a fighting chance," she said. She wished Phoenix could understand just how important that day's work was.

Before Cindy put Phoenix on the longe line, she put her through some stretching exercises she had learned during the years she was at Whitebrook.

"That looks interesting," Lonnie said from his office doorway.

Cindy looked up from where she was crouched in front of Phoenix. She held the filly's leg up by the knee, moving the leg in small circles.

"I'm just getting her joints warmed up," Cindy said, suddenly self-conscious with the trainer watching her.

"I didn't realize you were an equine massage therapist as well as a groom, a jockey, and a part-time trainer," Lonnie said. He watched for a minute longer, then shook his head. "I guess it can't hurt."

Cindy ignored his comment and put Phoenix on the longe line, jogging her first in one direction, then the other, before urging her to speed up to a canter. Phoenix snorted and tossed her head, giving a few playful bucks before settling down and moving easily at the end of the line.

"She's warm enough," Lonnie called out impatiently. "Get her saddled. I'll meet you at the track." He walked away, and Cindy put Phoenix in the crossties so that she could tack her up.

"You're going to fly for him, aren't you?" she murmured, checking the girth before she led Phoenix to the track, where a few late horses were still being worked.

"Don't expect too much," Lonnie said when Cindy

joined him. "I know you've put a lot into her, but she went lame so fast when we first brought her up here, I don't hold out a lot of hope. I've let you go this far only because you've been so determined to fix her."

"She's fine," Cindy said, hoping she was right. Lonnie gave her a boost onto Phoenix's back, and the filly craned her head around to sniff at the toe of Cindy's boot.

"Let's go," Cindy said, patting Phoenix's glossy neck.

"Take her around once at a jog, then halfway around at a canter," Lonnie said. "When you bring her around to the inside, run her for five furlongs. That'll give me a good sense of where she's at physically."

Cindy headed Phoenix clockwise on the outside rail, where the slower horses worked. She adjusted her reins, surprised to see her hands trembling a little. "I can't believe I'm nervous about a little breeze," she said to Phoenix. "We're going to be fine, aren't we?" Phoenix snorted with eagerness as they moved onto the rail. She danced excitedly, and Cindy smiled to herself. "*You're* going to be fine, anyway," she said, tightening her grip on the reins. "Just wait until we've jogged for a while. You'll get your chance to gallop."

Phoenix fought the pressure Cindy had on her mouth a little, but after a minute she settled down, and they completed a full circuit of the track at a slow jog.

Cindy opened the filly up to a controlled canter, keeping her on the left lead to protect her right leg.

"I know you can fly," Cindy said to Phoenix. "I just know you could blow all the other horses off the track."

When they turned to gallop along the inside rail, Phoenix nearly tore the reins from Cindy's hands in her excitement. Cindy felt something pop in her shoulder, and she gasped at the pain. "That wasn't good," she muttered to herself. But she couldn't stop now. Phoenix was eager to run. Cindy ignored the pain in her shoulder and crouched over the filly's shoulders, urging her to quicken her pace.

Running Phoenix at top speed reminded Cindy of all the reasons she loved to race. The wind whistled past her ears, and Phoenix's powerful strides gave her the sense that she really was flying. As they shot past the poles Cindy knew without a doubt that Phoenix was fast, very fast. If only the hot dagger of pain in her shoulder would go away, this would be the most perfect moment she'd had in a long time.

After they had passed the fifth furlong, Phoenix tried to keep running. It took all the strength Cindy had to slow her. When they came around to where Lonnie was waiting, the trainer's expression was neutral. "Let's take her back and check that leg over," he said.

"You saw her!" Cindy exclaimed, dismayed by his lack of excitement. "She's a bullet on the track. You have to let her race!"

Phoenix tossed her head and pranced as they left the track, and Lonnie rolled his eyes. "I can see how much she enjoyed it," he said. "But let's make sure her legs are okay before we start making big plans, okay?"

Cindy nodded, mollified.

"There's a race for maiden three-year-olds next week," Lonnie said. "It isn't a big purse, but it'll be a good test of her abilities. If the vet says she's sound, I'll enter her. Do you still want the ride?"

Cindy nodded. "Of course," she said firmly. "We'll do a great job, I'm sure of it."

Lonnie nodded slowly. "You'll get a chance to try, anyway," he said.

When he walked away, Cindy turned to Phoenix. "He just doesn't want to admit that he was wrong about you," she said, patting the filly's sweaty neck. "You're ready to race, aren't you?" Phoenix gazed at her with liquid brown eyes, and Cindy started to reach up to rub the filly's wind-tangled forelock, but a spasm of pain shot through her arm. She dropped it to her side and clenched her jaw, waiting for the pain to sub-side. "I just hope I can stay healthy enough to ride you."

After walking the filly until she was completely

81

cool, Cindy gave her a long bath, spending extra time soaking Phoenix's front leg before rubbing strong-smelling liniment into it and wrapping it again. "If this stuff didn't smell so nasty, I'd probably try it on myself," she said, eyeing the brown bottle. "But at least it seems to be helping you." When she put Phoenix in her stall, the filly was calm but bright-eyed.

"You liked being back on the track, didn't you?" Cindy said, pouring a measure of grain into Phoenix's feed pan. She patted the filly's glossy red-gold shoulder. "You're going to get your chance to race again."

When Cindy walked into the apartment later that afternoon, she was exhausted. Her shoulder throbbed angrily, and all she wanted to do was take some aspirin and lie down with an ice pack. She dropped her bag on the floor near the door and glanced at the stack of mail on the hall table, then noticed the blinking light on the answering machine.

When Cindy hit the play button, Ashleigh's voice came through the speaker.

"I'm bringing Honor Bright up to Belmont to race. There are a couple of good purses for four-year-old-and-up mares next month. One of them seems custom-made for her. Make sure you leave some time open for us!"

Cindy was smiling happily as she rewound the message. Soon she'd be riding one of her favorite horses on the Belmont track again. It was going to take everyone by surprise, but she would never turn down the chance to ride Honor in a race.

"I have Glitz ready for you," Matt said the next morning when Cindy arrived at the track. The gray colt stood in the crossties, wild-eyed, head high, prancing in place like a Lippizaner.

Cindy nodded, flexing her shoulder a little. Even after a night's rest and several doses of aspirin, she wasn't sure her shoulder was up to a work on Glitz. But she couldn't turn down the ride. Matt would want to know what was wrong. Rather than trying to explain, Cindy grabbed her helmet.

"Let's go," she said, leading the way to the track, while Matt followed with Glitz dancing at the end of his lead line.

When Matt released them onto the track, Glitz shied at everything that caught his eye, from a scrap of paper someone had dropped to the reflection of one of the track lights on the rail. Cindy headed the colt clockwise and kept him moving along the outside rail, struggling to hold the agitated Thoroughbred down to a jog. Glitz danced and tossed his head, trying to break free of the hold Cindy had on him. It took all her concentration to keep him under control.

Another horse and rider cantered by, sending Glitz

into a frenzy as he tried to run with the other horse. Cindy felt her shoulder give, and Glitz nearly got his head. Cindy struggled to regain control, finally stopping the colt by the rail and waiting for the pain in her shoulder to subside before she rode on. "Save it for a race," she said to the excited colt. "This is a workout, not the Kentucky Derby."

When she turned Glitz to gallop him along the inside rail, the colt pranced and snorted, fighting Cindy every step of the way. In the distance she heard shouting, but she was too busy trying to keep the fractious colt under control to pay any attention. She balanced over his shoulders as they passed the sixteenth-mile markers that lined the track, and Cindy fought the colt to keep him down to a steady gallop.

"Loose horse!" a voice bellowed over the loudspeakers. She looked up to see the track's red warning light, mounted on a pole in the infield, flashing to warn the exercise riders to clear the track because of a runaway. A chill of fear raced down Cindy's spine. She sat down in the saddle, hauling on Glitz's reins to slow him while she frantically looked around for a gap in the rail. They needed to get off the track!

Glitz jerked his head, and a streak of pain shot through Cindy's shoulder. For a moment the colt had his head, and he sped up again, nearly unseating Cindy. But she clung to his back and shortened the reins, trying not to panic as she struggled to get him back under control and out of harm's way. Finally he settled down, and Cindy glanced around, trying to spot the runaway animal. She looked for the nearest opening in the rail, berating herself for not paying better attention to the warning shouts. But Glitz had demanded every bit of her attention, and now she was in a dangerous position, galloping a headstrong horse while there was another thousand-pound animal racing mindlessly around the track.

Glitz was still galloping, and no amount of strength Cindy had could slow him down. From the corner of her eye she saw one of the outriders gallop his quarter horse along the outside rail. He was gesturing to her, and Cindy looked up, gasping in horror as she saw the riderless horse tearing blindly along the inside rail, heading directly toward them. Cindy's breath locked in her throat. She didn't know which way to turn Glitz to avoid running into the loose horse. She could see the wild look in the runaway's eyes and saw the lather flying from its coat as it thundered toward her. Cindy felt sick with fear, sure she wouldn't be able to get Glitz out of the path of the other horse.

Then she caught a blur from the corner of her eye as the outrider wheeled his stocky quarter horse and they charged across the track, cutting off the loose horse. As the outrider leaned forward and snagged the runaway's flapping reins, Cindy pulled Glitz to the right, toward the middle of the track, and was finally able to bring him to a stop.

Cindy felt her heart thud dully in her chest, and she exhaled slowly, weak with relief. That was the closest she had ever come to running into another horse, and she hoped the careless rider who had lost the horse would be banned from the track for good. If it hadn't been for the outrider's skillful work, the incident could have ended in disaster.

Shaken by the incident, Cindy was tempted to hand Glitz off to Matt and go back to the locker room, but she reminded herself that she was a professional. She took Glitz back to the outside rail and started to cool him down as the other exercise riders came back onto the track. In a minute the oval was back to normal, with horses jogging and galloping along the rails as though the near disaster had never happened.

That evening Cindy was in the kitchen slicing mushrooms for spaghetti sauce when the apartment door slammed shut. She hurried into the living room. Rachel was standing in the hallway, a glum look on her face.

"What's wrong?" Cindy asked.

"You were on the track with that loose horse today, weren't you?" Rachel asked, flopping onto the sofa.

Cindy nodded. "It was amazing that no one got hurt. I was sure Glitz and I were going to run right into that horse. It's a good thing that outrider was on the ball. I never did find out who the rider was who lost the horse. Everyone in the locker room said it was some careless bug."

Rachel dropped her gaze to her feet. "It was me," she said. "I was supposed to be on the runaway colt. I didn't have a good grip on the reins when I rode onto the track, and he dumped me before we even got started."

"Oh." Cindy stared at Rachel, who kept her eyes cast down.

"You don't have to say anything, Cindy," Rachel said. She looked up, her eyes filled with tears. "I've been suspended from riding indefinitely," she said. "The stewards said I'm not safe and I can't ride again until I'm able to pay full attention to my work."

Cindy nodded. She knew Rachel hadn't done it on purpose, and she was very lucky no one had been hurt by her carelessness.

"Matt was furious with me," Rachel said. "He told me I'm irresponsible and don't deserve to be around the horses. And he's right."

"At least no one got hurt," Cindy said, trying to feel some sympathy for her roommate.

"I know," Rachel said morosely. "Matt said the same thing. I need to make a decision about what my priorities are." She sank back and stared at the ceiling, sighing heavily. Then she swiped at her eyes with the back of her hand. "I'm sorry, Cindy. I wouldn't blame you if you never spoke to me again."

Cindy didn't know what she could say that would make Rachel feel better. Before she had known who was responsible for the loose horse, she had hoped the stewards would give the rider the worst punishment possible. Now that she knew whose fault it had been, she didn't know if she should feel any different.

The sound of the pot boiling over had Cindy hurrying back into the kitchen. By the time she returned to the living room, Rachel was in her bedroom with the door shut, a sign that she wanted to be left alone.

Rachel didn't leave her room for the rest of the evening. When Cindy went to bed, she could hear the muffled sound of sobbing coming from Rachel's room. Cindy sat up in bed, her diary on her lap, and recorded the events of the day.

I have never been so afraid as I was today when I saw that horse galloping toward Glitz and me. I should be furious with Rachel for letting it happen. But seeing how upset she is makes me feel bad for her. Besides, she isn't the only jockey who stays out late, then shows up at dawn for the works. They make it dangerous for everyone on the track. Just thinking about it makes me feel scared again. I have to stop replaying that moment in my head. Instead I'm going to lie down and think about riding Phoenix to a win next week. If I keep seeing that loose horse running toward me, I'm afraid I'll never go back on the track again.

IT'S RACE DAY, AND I WISH I WERE MORE EXCITED ABOUT TAK-
ing Phoenix onto the track. Even though she seems fine now,
I'm still worried about her leg. What makes me think I know
better than a big-time trainer like Lonnie? On top of that, no
matter how many times Rachel apologizes, I still can't get
the image of that horse running toward me out of my head. I
should have been more alert and more aware of what was
going on. The loose horse on the track may have been her
fault, but not realizing there was a problem until it was
almost too late was mine.

When Cindy arrived at the track the morning of
Phoenix's race, she was still a bundle of nerves. Doing
well that day meant more than winning a purse. It
could mean the difference between a good future for
Phoenix or a bleak one, and it was going to be a test of

her abilities as a jockey. She couldn't let her emotions ruin the race for her or for Phoenix.

"Just push her on through the race," Lonnie said, looking up from a copy of the track's condition book. "She's gotten used to favoring that leg, but don't let her. She's sound now." Cindy could see the page he was turned to, the one that described the race Phoenix was running. She had the information memorized. She and Phoenix were in the number four position, with a black filly named Flash 'n' Dash in the number three gate and a chestnut called Goforbroke in the number five spot. She had read the statistics on all the horses in the race. Phoenix's recorded breeze times were better than any of the other fillies', but the rest of them had run at least one other race. And according to the *Daily Racing Form*, Phoenix was the only one coming off an injury.

She nodded to Lonnie. "We'll do fine," she said. "I think we have a good chance."

Lonnie shrugged. "We'll see," he said. "I'll meet you at the saddling paddock."

Cindy stopped by Phoenix's stall on her way to the dressing room. The filly had her head out in the aisle, her ears were pricked, and her nostrils were flared.

"You know there's something going on, don't you?" Cindy asked her, rubbing Phoenix's glossy red-gold coat. Phoenix let out a piercing whinny. Cindy winced, then laughed. "I agree," she said. "We're going to sweep the field today, girl." She headed for the lockers, feeling a little better about the race. Phoenix was excited and eager, and Cindy knew she had to do her best to help the filly make a good showing.

But she was alarmed to feel her hands tremble slightly when she pulled on her gray-and-gold GeeGee silks. "It's a race," she scolded herself. "An easy race. Phoenix can handle it. You'll both be fine."

"Are you talking to yourself, Blake?" one of the other jockeys asked, glancing up from her seat on the bench. She tugged one of her boots on and frowned at Cindy. "Are you all right?"

Cindy stiffened her spine. "I'm fine," she said quickly, offering the sitting jockey a confident smile. But she was worried about Phoenix's leg and about her aching shoulder. Neither she nor the horse could afford to have a bad race that day.

Quit putting so much pressure on yourself, she said silently, frowning at her reflection as she checked her appearance in the mirror in the dressing room. She grabbed her racing saddle and left the locker room to weigh in with the clerk of the scales.

When it was time to head for the viewing paddock, Cindy followed the other jockeys through the tunnel. She eyed the other seven riders closely. She knew most of them. None was a very aggressive rider, and there were a couple of bugs who didn't have many races behind them. *It should be a very easy field,* she reassured herself, *as long as I don't let my nerves get the better of me.* She wished Ian were there to give her a few words of encouragement. She could have used some family support just then. But she was on her own, the way she had wanted to be. *I can handle this,* she told herself firmly, picking up her pace and trying to keep calm as she got closer and closer to the grandstand. She'd get Phoenix through the race with flying colors.

The horses circling the viewing paddock were all good-looking Thoroughbreds, but Cindy was sure none of them had Phoenix's heart. "You'll be fine," Lonnie said when she joined him at the number four spot, waiting for the groom to bring Phoenix around. "It's too bad Mrs. Goldrich won't be here to see her filly run."

Cindy nodded in agreement, but she was glad the owner wasn't there, just in case things didn't go well. *Stop thinking that way!* she ordered herself, but no matter how many times she tried to reinforce a positive state of mind, she kept imagining the worst.

When the handler stopped Phoenix in front of them, Lonnie gave Cindy a boost onto the filly's back, then stepped back. "Good luck," he said, tipping the brim of his baseball cap as Cindy collected her reins.

Cindy darted him a brief smile. "We'll do our best,"

she said as Phoenix was led off. "You're going to clean up out there today," she said to the filly, tucking her toes into the stirrups as the pony rider took the lead.

Phoenix pranced a little as they completed the post parade, and Cindy paid close attention to the filly's gait as they did their warm-up gallop. Phoenix's strides were even and strong, and from Cindy's position, she couldn't detect any sign of lameness. She patted Phoenix's glistening neck, encouraged by the ease of the filly's movements. Phoenix tossed her head, clearly eager to start running. Cindy smiled to herself. "You'll get your chance, girl," she said. "Save your energy for the race."

After the jostling behind the gate, the horses were soon loaded, and Cindy settled into position on Phoenix's back, prepared for the start. There was a tense moment of silence. Cindy crouched over the filly's neck, waiting for the starting bell. Around them horses shifted, snorted, and stamped nervously. After what felt like an eternity, the gate banged open. The horses leaped onto the track like a battalion charging in unison.

Phoenix was immediately boxed in, with no opening for an escape. Cindy felt as though she'd stepped into a nightmare. She ground her teeth in frustration as she took the filly to the rail, surrounded by slow horses and inexperienced jockeys. How could this be happening? Her worst fears were coming true. She glanced around, trying to find an opening to squeeze the filly through, but there didn't seem to be any clear way to get Phoenix out of the trap.

They covered the first furlong still boxed in by the other horses, and Cindy was worried that they might run the whole seven-furlong race in this formation.

When the filly to their right fell back, Cindy heaved a sigh of relief and started to move Phoenix toward the opening. But as they shifted toward the outside Cindy hesitated. Lonnie had told her that the vet said Phoenix's leg was as strong as it was going to get. Did that mean the filly was completely sound, or was there a chance she could break down? Cindy eyed the opening, wondering what the extra stress would do to Phoenix's already fragile leg. Taking her wide meant the filly would have to run farther, which would increase her chances of being injured.

While she was debating with herself, another two furlongs had passed. They were almost halfway through the race, and she wasn't helping Phoenix by riding timidly. Cindy hissed in frustration at her indecision. The middle of the race was not the time to start questioning the trainer.

But by the time she made up her mind to push the filly, they were coming into the turn. The horse to the inside had moved up to join the leaders, and the lead horse on the outside fell back a few steps. Once again

Cindy and Phoenix were blocked by slower horses, with no way to get past them.

When she caught a glimpse of space between the inside horse and the rail, Cindy urged the filly toward the hole. Phoenix started to move into the space, but the jockey on the horse in front of them moved closer to the rail, and Phoenix was forced to check her speed.

Before Cindy could make another move, the race was over. She brought Phoenix around and groaned when she saw the tote board. Phoenix had come in seventh in a field of eight. "It wasn't you," Cindy reassured the filly as they circled back toward the finish line. "I was too cautious. Lonnie will understand. He'll give you another chance. I'm sure of it."

But she wasn't at all sure what Lonnie would say about letting *her* race again—on Phoenix or any other horse in his stable.

Without a word to Cindy, Lonnie checked Phoenix's legs over. Still crouched by the filly's legs, he shook his head, then rose slowly and frowned at Cindy. "No heat, no apparent trauma. The filly seems to be in fine shape."

Cindy's sense of relief was short-lived.

"So if the filly is sound and you can get a good time out of her during a breeze, how do you account for such a dismal placing in the race?"

Cindy started to explain. She'd been tense because

of the close call with the runaway horse. She was worried about putting too much pressure on Phoenix. They'd had some bad luck when they broke from the gate. But she clamped her mouth shut. Everything she could possibly say sounded like a poor excuse. "I rode a bad race," she said honestly.

"After you cool her out, take her over to the veterinarian's barn," Lonnie told the waiting groom, handing Phoenix's lead line to the girl. When she walked away with the filly, Lonnie turned back to Cindy.

"I know you're dedicated to racing," Lonnie said. "But you need to have a lot more confidence when you're on the track. I don't run a second-rate facility, and I don't hire second-rate jockeys."

Cindy felt her hopes for a future at the track fade. Lonnie was right. She had ridden like a second-rate jockey that day.

"I'll give you one more chance on the track," he said. "But that's it. I'm not going to risk my reputation as a winning trainer by using a fainthearted jockey."

Cindy's heart soared. "I won't let you down," she said quickly. "I promise."

That night when she settled on her bed, an ice pack on her aching shoulder, Cindy flipped through an old album of photographs from Whitebrook. There was one of her with Glory, the gray stallion she had helped save, and one of her and Samantha with Sierra, the

Thoroughbred gelding Samantha and Tor had trained to steeplechase. She paused at a picture of her sitting on Champion, and a sob caught in her throat. She had been so sure of herself then, so brave and invincible. *I'll be that way again,* she told herself. *That's the only way I'll be able to succeed.* She closed the album and picked up her diary.

That had to be the absolute worst race of my life. I couldn't do anything right. My cautious riding may have kept Phoenix from hurting her leg, but it didn't do her any good, either. I wish I knew how to get my confidence back. I need it if I ever want to ride and win again.

8

RACHEL HAS BEEN GOING TO THE TRACK WITH ME EVERY MORN-
ing. She's working as a groom for Matt, Lonnie, and a couple
of other trainers. She seems pretty serious about getting her
license back. Maybe she's going to be okay. I wish I could say
the same for me.

Ashleigh will be here with Honor tomorrow. I'm excited
about seeing Honor again, but I'm not so sure I'm the best
jockey for her anymore. I wish I had a chance to race again
before I ride Honor. I'd still like to know that I can ride well,
especially after messing things up with Phoenix. But maybe
getting on a good horse that I've done well on in the past will
help me. At least Matt and Rachel are sticking by me. It is
good to have some friends I can count on.

"I want him to have a light workout today," Matt
said, holding Glitz's headstall while Cindy adjusted

her stirrups. "Tomorrow I'll have you breeze him so we can get a track time, and if it looks good, we're going to race him next week."

"Got it," Cindy said, gathering the reins and pointing Glitz toward the opening in the rail.

As she rode by Lonnie Gray, the trainer signaled to her. "When you're done today, come by my office," he said.

"Sure," Cindy said. "This is my last horse to work this morning. I'll be there as soon as I'm done."

"Good," he said. "I need to talk to you."

Cindy held Glitz at the rail and was about to ask Lonnie if there was a problem with Phoenix, but he turned his attention to one of his other colts that was coming off the track.

Glitz pranced, fighting to get moving, and Cindy was forced to concentrate on the gray colt. If there was a problem with Phoenix, she'd find out soon enough.

Cindy tried to keep her attention on Glitz as well as on the red warning light and the other riders on the track. But Glitz tossed his head and danced, requiring her to focus more on him and to stop flinching every time someone raised their voice or a horse galloped by. After several minutes she realized she had no choice but to quit worrying about possible disasters.

She smiled to herself. "I'm going to be okay," she

said, turning Glitz around when she was satisfied with his responsiveness. "Your owner is going to be so impressed when we show him how well you're doing."

At Cindy's cue, Glitz picked up his speed, moving into a smooth, powerful gallop. After putting the colt through his workout, Cindy returned him to the waiting groom.

"I can't believe he's the same out-of-control two-year-old we started with a couple of months ago," Matt said, scribbling notes on his clipboard. "He's ready to race. I wish you'd told me what a good jockey you are the day I met you. I feel like a jerk watching you ride so well out there."

"Thanks," Cindy said modestly, unfastening her chin strap. She reached up to pull her helmet off, wincing as her shoulder twinged painfully.

"Are you all right?" Matt asked, frowning at her.

"I'm fine," Cindy said, forcing a smile. "I just have some sore muscles."

"Get a massage," Matt said, looking back at his notes. "That'll loosen you up."

"That's a good idea," Cindy said. But she knew a massage wouldn't help the ache in her damaged shoulder joint.

"Will you be up to racing Glitz next week?" Matt asked.

"Of course," Cindy said without hesitation. She

certainly wasn't going to turn down any chance to race, especially not after her failure with Phoenix. She needed all the races she could get to show everyone what she could really do.

She left Glitz with Matt and the Stone Ridge groom and headed for the locker room. As soon as she took a couple of aspirin and had a long, hot shower, she would go find out what Lonnie wanted.

When she arrived at the GeeGee Stables area, Cindy strolled slowly past the stalls, admiring some of the best-bred horses on the East Coast. She paused at Phoenix's stall, where the filly was munching on a mouthful of hay. She looked fine, alert and bright-eyed. Cindy gave her soft nose a quick rub. "Are you all right?"

"I didn't want to talk to you about her," Lonnie said from his office doorway. He tilted his head toward another stall, where a black mare with a white star was tearing a bite of hay from the net in her stall. "It's about Midnight Rose."

Cindy had seen the big mare working on the track and was impressed with the way she moved. "What about her?" she asked, eyeing the mare curiously.

"One of my regular jockeys had a family emergency, and I need someone to race her this weekend. She's got a good chance of winning one of the four-

and-over mares' races on the Saturday program. I'd like to increase her earnings record before we retire her. It'll do a lot for the value of her foals."

"The third race on Saturday," Cindy said slowly. "That's the race with the big purse." After all her hard work to prove herself here, Lonnie was offering her one of his best mares in the same race Ashleigh had scheduled Honor to run in. Cindy couldn't believe her bad luck.

"That's the one," Lonnie said. "Do you want the ride? I'm offering you a second chance. I know you can ride well enough, and maybe on an experienced horse you'll manage the track a little better."

Cindy gazed around the stable, her eyes sweeping across the stalls filled with top-quality racehorses. She had assumed her second chance with Lonnie would be another race on Phoenix. But Midnight Rose was a proven horse. And racing for Lonnie would do her career a lot of good. She let out a groan of frustration. "I can't ride for you," she said. "I already have a horse for the race."

"Which one?" Lonnie asked, giving her a puzzled look.

"Honor Bright, for Whitebrook," Cindy replied, unable to keep a touch of pride from her voice.

"You're riding for Whitebrook?" Lonnie raised his

eyebrows. "Cindy, why would a farm like Whitebrook ask an untried jockey like you to ride one of their horses?"

Cindy stiffened. Lonnie was letting her ride for him because he felt sorry for her, not because he believed she was a capable jockey. She started to respond, then clamped her mouth shut. "I'll see you in the saddling paddock," she said stiffly, turning to stalk away.

When Ashleigh and Honor arrived later that afternoon, Cindy was at the back gate to greet them. She waited anxiously for Ashleigh to park the trailer. She hadn't seen the Whitebrook owner since she had taken Champion to Dubai. That had been over a year earlier. While she waited for Ashleigh to climb from the truck, Cindy relived that terrible moment when she had lost control of Champion and the stallion had run Ashleigh down. The accident had caused Ashleigh to lose her second child. Although Ashleigh had made it clear she didn't blame anyone, Cindy still felt responsible for what had happened that day, and she was more than a little nervous about seeing Ashleigh again.

But when Ashleigh came around the side of the trailer, she opened her arms to give Cindy an enthusiastic hug. "You look great!" she said, stepping back to smile warmly at Cindy.

Cindy sighed in relief at Ashleigh's friendly greeting. "You too," she said. "I'm so glad to see you."

"You can bring Honor out if you want," Ashleigh said, opening the trailer door so that Cindy could lead the chestnut mare down the ramp.

Cindy unclipped Honor's trailer tie, and Honor nuzzled her, blowing soft puffs of breath against her neck. Cindy smiled at the affectionate way Honor greeted her, and gave her nose a gentle rub. The scent and feel of the mare brought back lots of memories of riding Honor on the Whitebrook track, and the races they had run together. "Come on out, girl," she said, leading the mare into the sunlight. Honor raised her mahogany-colored nose and sniffed the air, whinnying loudly as she looked around.

"You've been here before," Cindy said, giving the mare's shoulder a pat. "She looks great," she told Ashleigh. "She should have a good race tomorrow. Do you want me to put her in her stall?"

"Sure," Ashleigh said, handing Cindy the paper with Honor's stall assignment on it. "I need to grab a few things, but then I'll be right there."

"I wish this race were happening later in the season," Cindy told Honor as she led the mare off. "You have a good chance of winning no matter who rides you. I'd still like to prove myself by my own talents." Honor nudged her nose against Cindy's shoulder, and

Cindy laughed. "But I would never, ever turn down a chance to ride you," she said, reaching up to rub Honor's glistening chestnut neck.

When Cindy reached the stall assigned to Whitebrook, she was surprised to see Tommy Turner there, reading through Belmont's current condition book. The paperback booklets, published by the track, contained details about all the races scheduled for each week.

Tommy, an experienced jockey, was well known around the track for his good sportsmanship and skillful riding. He always rode for the top stables at Belmont, Aqueduct, and Saratoga, then spent his winters in Florida for the racing season there. Cindy had talked to him only a few times, but Tommy was always polite and friendly, without the tough edge that some of the jockeys displayed.

Tommy looked up as Cindy stopped Honor in front of her stall. "Isn't that the Whitebrook mare?" he asked.

"She sure is," Cindy said, opening the door to Honor's stall. She rested a hand on Honor's shoulder. "Honor Bright is one of the farm's top mares."

"So this is my ride for tomorrow," Tommy said, looking closely at the dark chestnut mare.

"Your ride?" Cindy frowned, confused. She unclipped Honor's lead and stepped out of the stall.

Honor pushed her nose out the door as Cindy latched it. As Cindy turned to face Tommy, the mare nuzzled her shoulder, and Cindy automatically reached up to rub Honor's poll.

Tommy nodded. "Ashleigh Griffen called me a week or so ago and asked if I'd be available to ride this race for Whitebrook. I couldn't tell her no."

Cindy gaped at Tommy. "She asked you to ride Honor?"

"I'm looking forward to it," Tommy said. "Ashleigh and I raced against each other several times when I was starting out," he explained. "Between you and me, I was glad when she decided to retire." He grinned broadly. "She took a lot of wins away from me. Now it's my turn to win one for Whitebrook."

Tommy nodded toward Honor, who was snuffling at Cindy's hair. "How come you're handling the horse? Did you take a job as the mare's groom while she's here?"

"Ashleigh is on her way," Cindy said, still trying to absorb the news that Ashleigh had asked someone else to ride Honor.

"I see you two know each other."

At the sound of Ashleigh's voice, Cindy turned. She forced a weak smile. "It sounds like Honor has a good chance of winning her race with Tommy riding for you," she said.

"I was glad he was available," Ashleigh said, flashing a smile at Tommy. She frowned at Cindy. "Are you okay?"

"I'm going over to the kitchen to grab a cup of coffee," Tommy said quickly. "If you want to go over tomorrow's race with me, I can meet you there, Ashleigh."

"Great, Tommy," Ashleigh said. "I want to catch up on a few things with Cindy, and I'll be right over."

Tommy walked away, leaving Cindy and Ashleigh alone in front of Honor's stall.

Ashleigh pursed her lips. "I guess we had a miscommunication," she said, instantly guessing what was on Cindy's mind.

Cindy shrugged. "It's all right, Ashleigh. You didn't ask me to ride Honor in the first place. I just assumed I'd be racing her for you. It's great that Tommy is going to ride her. She has excellent odds of winning with him on board."

Ashleigh sighed. "I was going to ask you to ride for us, but from your letters, it sounded like you'd be too busy to take on another horse, and I didn't want to put you in the position of having to turn down a ride for one of the regular Belmont trainers." She smiled apologetically. "I asked Tommy to ride because I wanted a jockey who knows the track well, and one I could trust with Honor."

Cindy cringed inwardly. She hadn't wanted her family to worry about her, so she had made it sound as though she were getting in with a lot of the bigger barns. Ashleigh hadn't put her in a position to turn down a chance to race a good horse. She'd done that all on her own. Now she had to get back over to GeeGee and see if Lonnie would let her ride Midnight Rose. If she couldn't ride Honor, maybe she could prove herself by beating Tommy, who was an outstanding jockey, and Honor, who was an outstanding mare.

When Ashleigh headed for the track kitchen to discuss Honor's race with Tommy, Cindy hurried over to GeeGee Stables. But when she came around the corner of the shed row, she saw Lonnie talking to another jockey, Trevor Morris, and pointing at Midnight Rose. Cindy hesitated. When Trevor eyed the mare and nodded enthusiastically, she slipped away quietly. Obviously Lonnie had had no trouble finding a jockey willing to ride the mare.

She went back to Honor's stall and occupied herself grooming the Whitebrook mare, who seemed happy to have her company.

"I'm so dumb," Cindy groaned, dragging a brush down Honor's flank. "I really messed this one up, girl. But," she added, "I know you'll do great on the track with Tommy." She sighed. "I'll just have to watch from the rail."

The following morning, while Ashleigh took care of Honor's tack, Cindy groomed the mare until her coat gleamed like a new penny and then combed her silky mane and tail smooth. "I'll lead her to the saddling paddock," she told Ashleigh, who nodded.

"Thanks for being such a good sport about this, Cindy," she said as they left the stable. "I know you must be disappointed that you aren't the one riding her."

"It's okay," Cindy said with a shrug. "I've had some great races on Honor." She led Honor into the saddling paddock, and they waited for Tommy to come up from the jockeys' lounge with his saddle. They quickly tacked the mare up, and Ashleigh went into the viewing paddock to wait with Tommy while Cindy walked Honor out for the spectators to see.

After Tommy settled onto Honor's back, Cindy led them to the track opening. She gave Tommy a thumbs-up as he rode onto the track. "Good luck," she called, wishing with all her heart that she were riding. She joined Ashleigh at the rail, and they waited in tense silence for the race to start.

"And the-e-ey're off!"

At the announcer's cry, Cindy craned her neck, keeping her eyes glued to Honor. She heard Ashleigh beside her, calling instructions to Tommy as if he could hear her. Cindy almost laughed aloud. Tommy did

110

exactly what Ashleigh wanted done. Cindy realized as she watched the race that Tommy was making the same moves she would make if she was riding boldly.

Midnight Rose made a good showing, fighting Honor for first place. The black mare and the chestnut mare stayed stride for stride from the first furlong right to the finish line.

"Go!" Cindy screamed at Honor, gripping the rail, leaning forward as if she could push the mare into a faster gait. Tommy rode skillfully, and at the last minute he shifted subtly, letting Honor find the last bit of speed she needed to sweep across the finish line in first place.

"Wow!" Ashleigh gasped, turning to Cindy with a broad smile. "Did you see that? Honor is still full of fire!"

"I saw," Cindy said, happy for Whitebrook and for Tommy, and wishing it didn't bother her that she hadn't been the one to win the race for Ashleigh.

That evening when Cindy curled up on her bed, warm light glowed from her brass table lamp, which she had polished until it shone like gold. She pulled her diary from the top drawer of her dresser, leaned back against the headboard, and began to write.

I really blew it. I never even asked about riding for Whitebrook. I just assumed they wanted me to, but I should have talked to Ashleigh before I turned Lonnie down. This certainly didn't turn out the way I had expected it to. I'm so happy Honor won her race, but after watching Tommy ride, I know I could have done what he did. I hope Lonnie will give me another chance to ride for him, but I wouldn't blame him if he didn't.

9

*SEEING ASHLEIGH AND HONOR MADE ME HOMESICK. I WON-
der if I should just pack up and go home. I haven't done anything spectacular since I got to New York. It would be nice
to be back at Whitebrook. But I can't leave Phoenix. I'd feel
like I was deserting her. If Lonnie will let me race again, I
know I can do a better job.*

"When are you coming back to Kentucky for a
visit?" Ashleigh asked Cindy. They were standing by
the Whitebrook truck at the track's back gate. Honor
was already loaded and ready for the trip home.
"Kevin and Christina are starting riding lessons. You
have to see them on their ponies."

"I'll bet they're both too cute for words." Cindy
smiled at the thought of her little brother wearing
jodhpurs and a black helmet, sitting on a stubby-

legged pony. "Are you training them both to be jockeys?" she asked jokingly.

Ashleigh shook her head. "An old friend of mine, Mona Gardener, has opened a riding academy. I think it will be easier for Christina and me if she takes lessons from someone else. She may be only five, but she sure has a mind of her own." She looked hard at Cindy. "A lot like someone else I know."

Cindy wrinkled her nose at Ashleigh. "You do mean yourself, right?"

"You know I mean you," Ashleigh said with a laugh.

"I don't know when I'll get home," Cindy said. "I can't afford to take much time off. There are a lot of jockeys looking for work around here. I don't want to miss out on any rides."

"I understand," Ashleigh said. She gave Cindy a long look. "Just let me know if you want some references."

Cindy shook her head firmly. "I'm doing great, honestly. But thanks for offering."

She and Ashleigh hugged briefly, then Cindy watched Ashleigh drive out of the back gate before she turned to walk back to the barns.

Matt waved her over to his office as she passed the Stone Ridge stabling area. "I named you to ride Glitz in a race for maiden two-year-olds the day after tomorrow," he said.

"Thank you, Matt," Cindy said. If she won on Glitz, that would certainly help her reputation.

"Rachel has been granted track privileges again," Matt said. "I'm going to let her start working Moon Shadow. They get along, and she seems able to handle him on the track."

Cindy nodded. Rachel had worked hard to restore her credibility with the track officials. "I'm sure she'll do well with him."

"She's taking her job here a lot more seriously," Matt said. "I think losing her apprentice license for a few weeks was a good thing. It sure made her think about what was important to her."

The day of Glitz's race, it started raining early in the morning. After working her horses, Cindy changed into dry clothes. She pulled the hood of her slicker over her head when she stepped outside the jockeys' locker room and went in search of Matt. She found him in the track kitchen, having coffee with Rachel.

"We haven't worked Glitz on a wet track," Cindy said, worried. "Are you sure you still want to race him today?"

"We have to," Matt said. "The owner is in town for the day, and he wants to see his colt in a race."

"Okay," Cindy said reluctantly. "I just hope he can handle the sloppy conditions."

"It's only drizzling," Matt reassured her. "It's supposed to dry out by this afternoon. The track should be fine."

The sun finally peeked out from behind the clouds at noon, but the track was a sodden mess. The track crew dragged the surface smooth, and the special footing helped the water drain away from the top, but they couldn't dry the dirt. In spite of the crew's hard work, the track's surface was like wet cement.

Cindy watched the first two races on the television in the lounge. The horses coming off the track were mud-spattered and wet, and the jockeys looked as though they had been rolling on the track instead of riding horses on it. She went to the locker room to change into her silks, then stood in front of the mirror, smoothing down her clean racing shirt.

"Enjoy the clean look," another jockey said, coming in from a race. "In a few minutes you're going to look just like me."

Except for where her goggles had covered her face, the woman was brown with mud. She grinned at Cindy, her teeth white against the darkness of her filthy skin. Globs of mud clung to her white pants, and her shirt was so dirty, it was difficult to tell what color her silks were.

"Don't use up all the hot water," Cindy joked as the other jockey headed for the showers. Cindy left the locker room and headed for the saddling paddock, her helmet under her arm.

Glitz's owner, Mr. Jacobs, was a heavyset middle-aged man. He was dressed in a dark suit, complete with a silver tie. He smiled broadly at Cindy when she met him at the viewing ring.

"Matt says you've worked wonders with my colt," he said, shaking Cindy's hand. "I can hardly wait to see how he does on the track."

"I hope we'll do a good job for you," Cindy said, glancing toward the track, where the grounds crew was smoothing the surface before the race.

"Well, good luck out there," Mr. Jacobs said heartily.

"Thanks," Cindy said. She knew she was going to need more than just luck that day. A green horse on a wet track was a bad combination. She clenched and released her hands as she stood on the number four spot, waiting for Matt to bring Glitz around so she could mount up.

"Scared?" one of the other jockeys, Joe Thurman, asked her. Joe was waiting at the number five spot for his ride. The experienced jockey looked relaxed and confident.

Cindy stiffened at his words. She wasn't scared.

She was fine. She could handle Glitz, and she could handle a sloppy track. Still, she told herself, she was right to feel concerned about the track conditions and the unproven colt she was racing. She wanted to win; she just wanted to do it safely.

"No, I'm not scared," she said, trying to sound sure of herself. "I'm going to have a great time out there today. I like playing in the mud."

"I'm sure you'll be seeing plenty of it flying off the hooves of the horses in front of you," Joe said. He stepped forward as the horses came around the ring. When the handler stopped Joe's ride, a powerful-looking gray colt, the jockey grabbed the reins and vaulted lightly onto the horse's back. Cindy watched him ride away, then turned as Matt stopped Glitz in front of her.

Glitz pranced against the hold Matt had on his lead and darted looks right and left. He whinnied loudly, dancing his hindquarters around as he fought to get on the track and start moving.

"You'll be fine," Matt said, giving Cindy's shoulder an encouraging squeeze before offering her a leg up. Soon Cindy and Glitz were part of the post parade, passing in front of the grandstand on the way to the gate. Because of the mud flying off the horses' hooves, most of the spectators had retreated from the rail and were watching from under the covered grandstand.

When Glitz was loaded into his slot, Cindy inhaled and exhaled slowly and deeply, knotting her fingers in the colt's gray mane. She braced herself for the start, swallowing a lump of nerves that seemed to be stuck in her throat. Glitz had calmed down now that he was in the gate, and Cindy hoped he stayed that way. At that moment she didn't care about winning the race. She just wanted to get through it in one piece.

But when the horses came out of the gate, Glitz broke too fast for the wet track. His hooves tore at the heavy footing, and he nearly went down before the race even started.

By the time Cindy got him under control and running, the wall of horses in front of them was leaving a torrent of mud in its wake. Joe Thurman's words about being sprayed with mud echoed in Cindy's head. She clenched her teeth and pushed the colt on, trying to ignore the sting of the debris flying off the lead horses' hooves.

Cindy had to peel off her dirty goggles before they completed the first furlong. In spite of the difficult conditions, Glitz ran gamely, and Cindy was proud of the effort he put into the race. She rubbed the colt's mud-spattered neck with her knuckles.

"You're doing fine, boy," she muttered, careful not to open her mouth very much as she offered Glitz a few words of encouragement. She didn't want a mouthful of mud.

But the horses running ahead of them were churning up the track, leaving poor footing behind them. Another colt crowded next to Glitz, nearly sending him into the rail. The gray colt faltered, but he managed to keep his feet under him and kept on running. Cindy breathed a shaky sigh and urged him on. *You need to be gutsy*, she ordered herself. *Ride like you have no fear!*

"Attaboy," she said to the colt, pressing her hands up onto his neck. Glitz battled his way through the sticky footing to catch up with the lead horses. As they closed on the front-runners, Cindy looked for an opening in the line of racing Thoroughbreds. She pulled her second pair of dirty goggles down, leaving them dangling around her neck. Through her last clean pair of goggles, she spotted a sliver of space between two horses and drove Glitz toward the tiny opening.

But as they made their move one of the horses threw a huge clod of dirt up with his hooves. It smacked Glitz's poll and sent a spray of mud into Cindy's face, splattering her goggles and blinding her. At the same time she felt Glitz jerk his head up. He floundered as he lost his pace, and Cindy knew they were going to go down. *At least the main field is well ahead of us, so we won't be trampled by the racing horses,* she thought as she sailed over the colt's shoulder.

That thought was small comfort when she landed with a jolt on her bad shoulder, then rolled several times in the muck before finally coming to a stop. The breath had been knocked out of her, and Cindy lay on her back, gazing up at the sky while she struggled to inhale. She was still too stunned by the landing to tell if she had hurt herself seriously.

She wasn't sure how many seconds passed before the first emergency workers were hovering over her. A narrow-faced medic with piercing brown eyes kept asking silly questions that Cindy knew were intended to see if she had a concussion.

"What is your name?"

"I'm fine," she snapped. She didn't want to lie there in the sloppy mud answering questions. She wanted to get off the track and go clean up. "My name is Cindy Blake, it's the second weekend of May, and my head is just dandy."

But as she started to sit up, Cindy fell back with a groan. "I think I wrenched my shoulder a little, though," she said, feeling dizzy as a wave of pain swept over her.

"Just stay still," the medic ordered.

Cindy hated feeling so helpless, but when she tried to move again, another wave of pain stopped her, and she lay quietly, waiting for the ambulance crew to take care of her.

The medics gently slid her onto a stretcher. "How is my colt?" she asked, trying to twist around to get a glimpse of Glitz before they put her into the waiting ambulance.

"They loaded him into a van to take him off the track," one of the medics said. "It didn't look good."

Cindy sank back onto the gurney and bit her lower lip. She had let Matt push her to ride the colt, even though she had known it was a bad idea. If Glitz didn't make it, she would never forgive herself.

She was held overnight at the hospital. "For observation," the doctor had said firmly when she told him she wanted to leave. When Cindy finally got home, Rachel fussed over her like a mother hen over a chick. Cindy was glad to go to bed to get some peace and quiet. Finally, in the solitude of her bedroom, she got out her diary to make an entry.

They did a scan of my head and shoulder at the hospital. The doctor said my helmet did its job protecting me, but my shoulder took a beating. He asked about the old fracture from when I came off Honor at the Whitebrook practice track. I told him that was years ago. He said breaks heal, but without proper therapy and rest, damaged tendons and ligaments have to be repaired surgically. He said if I don't treat my shoulder right, I could end up crippled. I don't know what to do anymore. I've only managed to ride in two races since I've been at Belmont, and they've both been terrible. Maybe the sheik was right all along. I have no talent. I've just been lucky. Until now.

10

I'VE BEEN STUCK WEARING A SLING FOR THREE WEEKS, AND THE doctor says that after another week of keeping my shoulder immobile, he'll approve me to ride again. Glitz tore some muscles in his shoulder. He's off the track for the rest of the season, but it could have been a lot worse.

Glitz's owner, Mr. Jacobs, told me he felt responsible for what happened, because he insisted on seeing Glitz race that day. That makes me feel a little better.

"Are you sure you'll be ready to race in another week?" Lonnie asked, gesturing toward the sling that supported Cindy's shoulder.

"Positive," she said. "Have you decided what you're going to do with Phoenix?" She bit her lower lip, waiting anxiously to hear what the trainer had to say.

Lonnie looked down at the paperwork on his desk.

124

"She seems sound enough," he said. "Mrs. Goldrich will be here in a few weeks, so I think we'll put Phoenix on the track and let her owner decide what she wants to do."

"And I'm going to ride her, right?" Cindy held her breath, waiting for Lonnie's response.

He looked up slowly, his mouth pinched into a thin line. Cindy knew Lonnie had lost a lot of respect for her in the past month. First she had raced Phoenix badly, then she had told him she couldn't ride Midnight Rose when she really could have, and now she was walking around in a sling after taking a fall in the only other race she'd ridden at Belmont. Cindy wouldn't have been surprised if Lonnie told her to get lost.

Lonnie sighed. "Well, I told you I'd give you a second chance, didn't I?" He raised his hands in surrender. "You can ride Phoenix one more time. But that'll be your last chance, okay?"

"Thank you," Cindy said, relieved. "You won't be sorry."

She headed for Stone Ridge. Moon Shadow was in the aisle, and Rachel looked up from running a brush along his flank. "Did you come to watch us race this afternoon?" she asked.

Cindy nodded. "I'm the official Rachel Daniels cheering section," she said with a grin.

When Rachel rode Shadow onto the track, Cindy stood at the rail with Matt. Shadow pranced past the grandstand, his neck arched and his tail high. Rachel nodded toward Cindy, smiling brightly.

When the race started, Cindy watched closely as Rachel guided Shadow to the rail with the rest of the field. "Don't get boxed in," she muttered, her eyes fixed on Rachel and Shadow.

She relaxed a little when Rachel rated the colt, holding him back. Matt inhaled sharply, but Cindy nodded in approval. "Smart move, Rachel," she murmured. "He has plenty of stamina. He'll make it up at the end."

As the lead horses began to lose their momentum, Rachel brought Shadow to the outside and moved around the slowing horses, holding him at a steady pace, passing horse after horse to move to the lead. As the field bore down on the finish line, Moon Shadow was ahead by several lengths, and Cindy screamed herself hoarse as Rachel stood in the saddle and waved to the cheering crowd.

"Congratulations," Cindy said, grinning at Matt, who looked stunned.

"They won," he said, staring at the placings on the board. "Rachel and Moon Shadow won!"

"They're waiting for you at the winner's circle," Cindy said, giving Matt a gentle shove in the right direction. She stood outside the circle and watched proudly while Matt and Rachel posed for the photographer.

"You're going to lose your bug by the end of the summer," Cindy predicted when Rachel came home that evening.

"I hope so," Rachel said. She pointed at an open cookbook on the kitchen counter. "Are you getting so bored at home that you're teaching yourself to cook?"

Cindy glanced at the mess she had made of the kitchen and wrinkled her nose. "I thought it might be fun to eat something besides canned soup," she said. "I'm fixing spinach lasagna tonight."

"That sounds really good," Rachel said. "It's too bad I'm going to miss it, but Matt invited me out for a victory dinner. In fact," she said, glancing at the kitchen clock, "I need to get ready to go. He told me to dress up. We're going to a nice restaurant."

"Have fun," Cindy said. She was glad Rachel and Matt were getting along so well, but once again she thought of Ben. Cindy grabbed the bag of spinach from the counter and dumped the leaves into the sink to wash them. Thinking about Ben wouldn't do her any good. She concentrated on preparing her lonely dinner, determined not to let thoughts of Dubai, Ben, or even Champion haunt her.

. . .

The morning after the doctor cleared her to ride again, Cindy woke up earlier than usual. She dressed quickly and hurried to the track, eager to get back in the irons once more.

Cindy's first stop was at Phoenix's stall. The filly was still dozing, but she caught Cindy's scent and her eyes opened. She flared her nostrils, pushing her nose over the stall's half door.

"Look," Cindy said to the chestnut filly, running a hand along Phoenix's warm neck while she held up the doctor's clearance. "I can ride you again. Isn't that cool?" Phoenix nosed Cindy's hands, sniffing at the paper, then snorted and tossed her head.

Cindy puckered her mouth. "You'd be happy to see anyone who would feed you, wouldn't you?" But when she rubbed Phoenix's forehead, the filly craned her neck so that Cindy could reach the hollow at her throat, and she grunted softly when Cindy obliged by rubbing the filly's sleek throat for a minute.

"There," she said, dropping her hand. Phoenix, awake now, shook herself thoroughly, starting with her head and ending with a flick of her tail. After a big yawn, she checked Cindy over once more, searching for food.

"You can have a nice, all-over grooming after we put you through your exercises this morning," Cindy informed her. "Then you can have breakfast. You know the routine."

She glanced at her watch, surprised at the amount of time she had spent petting Phoenix.

Phoenix's groom would be coming soon to prepare her for her work, so Cindy hurried between the shed rows to Stone Ridge Stables.

"Good to have you back," one of the grooms called as she strode by a row of stalls. Cindy waved, smiling.

"Welcome back," one of the other jockeys said, nodding to Cindy as she hurried by. She was greeted by numerous people she hadn't seen in the last several weeks. By the time she reached Stone Ridge, Cindy felt pretty good. The warm welcome she had gotten made her feel she really was a part of the backside crowd.

Matt was sitting in his combination office and feed room when Cindy got to the Stone Ridge stable area. Cindy hadn't been in the office since getting hurt. She noticed that Matt's card table had been replaced with a real desk, and he was sitting in an executive-style chair instead of his old folding chair.

"This looks nice," she said approvingly, looking around the organized room.

Matt grinned. "I invested a little of the purse from Rachel and Moon Shadow's win last week," he said proudly, encompassing the room with a sweeping motion. "I think it makes the stable look a lot more professional."

"Rachel is still all bubbly about the win," Cindy said.

"Me too," Matt said with a grin. "How's the shoulder?" he asked, nodding at Cindy's arm.

Cindy raised her arm and waved it, grinning confidently. "It feels great," she said. "I'm ready to get to work."

"It's really good to have you back." Matt glanced down at the paperwork on his desk, then looked up at Cindy again. He rubbed his chin with his thumb. "I've decided to let Rachel keep working with Moon Shadow and Current Event," he said. "He'll be ready to race soon. It wouldn't be right to take either of them away from her now, after all the work she's done."

Cindy nodded in understanding. Rachel had worked hard to restore her credibility as a jockey.

"But I'd still like you to work Falcon," Matt added. "She should be ready to race soon."

"Thanks," Cindy said. Racing Falcon was the perfect opportunity to show everyone that she was healthy and ready to work.

By the time Falcon was saddled and ready for her work that morning, the track was busy. Several more jockeys and trainers greeted Cindy warmly, and she rode onto the track with a smile on her face. Falcon listened to Cindy's cues and stayed on the rail. Other riders thundered by on the inside rail, galloping their horses, and the sound of hooves pounding the track, the heavy breathing of the working horses, and the smell of the sweating animals made Cindy feel at home. In spite of all the activity on the track, Falcon kept to an easy jog, not fighting Cindy at all. Cindy rubbed the filly's smooth neck as they circled the track. It felt wonderful to be on a horse again. The muscles in her shoulder strained a little against the pull on the reins, but she ignored the tight feeling. She was sure the muscles would be stretched out and limbered up again in no time.

After putting Falcon up, Cindy made the rounds of the stables, letting trainers know she was cleared to ride again. By the time she headed for Lonnie Gray's office to discuss Phoenix's prerace training, she had several horses to work. It felt good to have trainers asking her to exercise their horses. Maybe things were going to be okay after all.

Cindy still worried about Phoenix's future. If she didn't come through with a spectacular display in her race, Lonnie would certainly recommend that her owner get rid of the filly. According to Lonnie, Gloria Goldrich bought and sold horses all the time, only holding on to the ones that won races.

"Cindy!"

She was almost to Phoenix's stall when she heard her name. She turned to see Lonnie Gray striding down the aisle toward her.

"Hi," she said.

"I saw you on the track," he said. "I'm glad to see you're ready to work again." He tilted his head toward Phoenix's stall. "Are you ready for your race with Phoenix?"

Cindy nodded slowly. "She looks ready to run," she acknowledged. "Did you have a race in mind?"

"I need to discuss that with Mrs. Goldrich," Lonnie replied. "She wants to be here to see the filly run, remember."

That night when she went to bed, Cindy got her diary out. She glanced through some of the earlier entries, surprised to realize that she had been back in the United States for almost a year. And she still was nowhere near where she wanted to be. She uncapped her pen and began to write.

I'm so glad things are going well for Matt and for Rachel. Now it's my turn for some good luck. I hope that when Mrs. Goldrich sees me race her filly, she will be so impressed with Phoenix's heart and determination that she'll want to keep her on the track. And I'm sure Falcon will do a great job in her first race, too. Things are going to get better from now on, I'm sure of it.

11

LONNIE STILL HASN'T SETTLED ON A RACE FOR PHOENIX. HE told me I'll be the first to know. Meanwhile, I've been riding Falcon almost every day. She's definitely ready to race. Matt has been reviewing the schedules trying to find a good race for her, one she'll have a good chance of winning.

Cindy glanced at the glowing numbers on her bedside clock radio and jumped up, snapping her diary shut. She dressed quickly, then filled her commuter mug with coffee and headed for the track.

"I talked to Mrs. Goldrich about Phoenix," Lonnie told Cindy when she got to the barn. "She's had a change of plans. She won't be able to make it to the track, and she told me to put the filly in a claiming race."

Disappointment settled on Cindy like a dark cloud. The rules of a claiming race were that horses could be purchased out of a race for a specified amount of money, so any owner or trainer registered with the Thoroughbred Association could put a claim on Phoenix. Without any winnings to her credit, she would go into a low-priced claiming race, which meant an uncertain future for her. If she ran poorly or broke down again, Phoenix wouldn't be claimed at all. She could end up going to the dog food buyer at auction—which was the same terrible outcome Cindy had worked so hard to prevent.

"Doesn't Mrs. Goldrich care about her horse at all?" she asked. "Why can't you give Phoenix one more chance?"

"I don't have a choice," Lonnie said. "Mrs. Goldrich wants her gone. The best I could do was to talk her into entering the filly in a claiming race. Phoenix blew her last race. Her owner wanted her to go straight to auction."

Cindy went rigid. "Phoenix didn't blow that race," she said sharply. "I did. I rode her too cautiously." She felt sick. She had let the filly down.

"Some stable that isn't quite as well known as ours might be very happy with her," Lonnie said.

Cindy wanted to argue. But she couldn't force Lonnie to change his mind or get him to change Mrs. Goldrich's.

"I still want to ride her," she said. She had held the filly back in the last race because she was afraid. But Phoenix was fine. Cindy was sure that if she let her run, they could win this time. At least that would make the filly more valuable to whoever claimed her and give her a better chance at a good life.

When Cindy went to the track kitchen at lunchtime, Rachel rushed up to the table. She was bubbling with excitement. "I've got some great news," she said, sitting down across from Cindy.

"That's nice," Cindy said distractedly, taking a bite of her salad. Her mind was on Phoenix and what she needed to do to help the filly run a successful race. *What she needs is a jockey who isn't going to coddle her*, Cindy berated herself. *A confident jockey who's going to treat her like a healthy, capable racehorse.*

A flash of light caught Cindy's eyes. She blinked, her attention finally on the source of the twinkle, and gaped at Rachel's hand as her roommate moved her finger so that more sparkles danced off the diamond on her finger.

"What's that for?" Cindy asked, eyeing the ring on Rachel's left hand.

"Haven't you ever seen an engagement ring before?" Rachel held her hand out, flaunting the gold ring with its tiny diamond. "Isn't it perfect? It's only a little stone, but Matt gave it to me, and that's all that matters." She grinned happily. "Right now all the money has to go to the horses." She laughed. "Matt says he has to work twice as hard so he can afford his horses' lifestyle."

Cindy stared at Rachel. "You're going to be eating, sleeping, and breathing horses twenty-four hours a day," she said in a warning voice. "Are you ready for that?"

"I'll be working with someone I love," Rachel said, beaming. "This is what I've always dreamed of." She gazed down at the ring on her finger. "Finding someone that I could be a partner with. We're going to make a great team."

"Then I'm really happy for you," Cindy said, smiling at her friend. "You're lucky," she said. "Matt's a great guy." So why did she feel a little sad to see Rachel so happy about being engaged to Matt? A serious relationship wasn't something Cindy herself was looking for. She wanted to race, and with the time she put into working, she didn't have any left for a friendly date with one of the guys around the track, much less a boyfriend.

Besides, she told herself, *look what happened with Ben. I thought he was a great guy, but I was wrong. Anyway, I don't need anyone. I have the horses, and that's enough.*

"Matt's looking for you, by the way," Rachel said, standing up.

Cindy nodded. "I'll head over to the stable as soon

as I finish my lunch, " she said. Rachel walked away with a bounce in her step.

When Cindy reached the edge of the shed row where Stone Ridge's stabling area was located, she saw Matt standing in front of Falcon's stall. Cindy watched Matt give the chestnut filly's nose a rub. Then his shoulders sagged and he shook his head slowly, turning away from the stall.

Cindy frowned. Something was bothering Matt. She strode along the aisle, and Matt turned to face her. His worried expression vanished, and Cindy wondered if she had misread him.

"I'm glad you're here," he said. "I'm entering Falcon in a race and I want you to ride her." Even though his face looked calm, his voice had an edge to it. Something was definitely wrong. Cindy felt a twinge of concern for her friend.

"Of course I'll ride her," she said. "When is the race?"

When Matt told her, Cindy frowned at him, dismayed. "But that's a claiming race," she protested. "Why are you doing that?"

Matt looked down at the floor of the aisle, then back up at Cindy. "I need money for a down payment on a little farm I found," he said. "I'm going to keep Moon Shadow and take on a couple more horses for other owners."

"But why Falcon?" Cindy frowned at him. "She was going to be your ticket to fame and fortune, remember?"

"I can make more money right away on stud fees from Moon Shadow than on Falcon's purses and future foals," he said. "Right now Falcon is the most expendable horse I have. It's a practical business decision."

"Right," Cindy said, thinking of the ring glittering on Rachel's finger. "Does Rachel know you're doing this?" she asked.

Matt shook his head. "I want to surprise her," he said.

Cindy raised her eyebrows. "I think selling Falcon will be a big surprise," she said dryly.

Matt ignored her comment. "Will you ride her for me?"

Cindy sighed. "I can't, Matt."

"But you have to," he said. "You've been riding her consistently, and the two of you work well together. You're my best chance for a win."

"I already committed to ride another horse." Cindy thought of Phoenix and their first, horrible race. She had to make it up to the filly. "Maybe Rachel could ride Falcon," she suggested.

Matt shook his head. "She doesn't handle her nearly as well as you do," he countered. "What other horse did you commit to?"

Cindy grimaced. "The filly I've been working with for GeeGee Stables," she said.

"Lonnie Gray can hire another jockey," Matt said. "GeeGee Stables can pick anyone they want to race their horses. I can't. I need you, Cindy. Falcon needs you."

"I can't," Cindy said miserably. "I just can't, Matt."

She walked away, unable to shake the feeling that she was letting her best friends down.

That evening Rachel stood in the middle of the apartment's tiny living room, glaring at Cindy. Cindy sat on the sofa, her elbows resting on her thighs, her hands hanging limp between her knees.

"How could you tell Matt no?" Rachel demanded. "After everything he's done for you? I can't believe you're letting him down like this, Cindy."

"I can't help it," Cindy said unhappily. "I have to keep my promise to Phoenix."

"But if Falcon does well in this race, Matt could attract some other owners. With the purse money, he could afford to pick up another colt."

Cindy frowned. Apparently Rachel still didn't know that Matt had entered Falcon in a claiming race. How could he keep that a secret? Eventually she was going to look at a condition book, and she'd see for herself. But Cindy clamped her mouth shut. It was up to Matt to tell Rachel, not her. She only hoped it didn't backfire on him. She sighed, thinking of Ben again and how much he had hurt her feelings by not being honest with her. She hated to think of how upset Rachel was going to be with Matt when she found out the truth.

Cindy sighed, rubbing her face with her hands. "I'm not doing it to hurt Matt, Rachel." Cindy had a horrible feeling that because of her decision, she was going to lose Rachel as a friend. "I'm sure you could handle her in the race," she said, feeling desperate. "You're a good jockey, Rachel."

"But you always seem to know what she's going to do before she does it," Rachel said. "Matt is counting on that."

Which was exactly why she had to ride Phoenix. No one else had spent the time with the chestnut filly that she had. No one else had raced her, and no one else was going to. Cindy had to ride Phoenix. She didn't have a choice.

"I'm sorry, Rachel," Cindy said. "I can't."

Rachel spun around and stalked out of the apartment, her back rigid and her head held high.

That night when Cindy opened her diary, she was surprised at how many entries she had made in it. "Here's one more," she murmured, pressing her pen to the top of the page.

I must be out of my mind. I'm turning down a chance to ride Falcon in order to race Phoenix. I don't even know if she'll be able to finish the race. Rachel is furious with me, and I know I'm letting Matt down. But I can't turn my back on Phoenix. She trusts me, and I made a promise to her. Why is everything always so hard?

12

Rachel hasn't been around the apartment much the last few days. I've seen her on the track, working Falcon for Matt, but I haven't had a chance to talk to her. Phoenix is always so happy to see me when I go to the barn. The vet says her leg is in great shape, so I can't use that as an excuse to baby her during the race. I have to race her as though she's the soundest horse on the track. And I have to work the field like I'm the best jockey out there, too.

It was late afternoon when Cindy opened the door to Phoenix's stall and slipped inside. After a good workout early in the morning, Phoenix's groom had bathed her and rewrapped her legs.

"Next weekend, girl," she said, running her hand along the filly's sleek neck. She smiled sadly. "At least I bought you a little time, and no one can say you're lame now. If all goes well, someone will recognize your qualities and you'll end up at a nice breeding farm." The filly nuzzled her affectionately, and Cindy absently rubbed her smooth brown nose.

"I guess I'd better start apartment hunting," she said. "I'm going to do everything I can to help you win, and if we succeed, Rachel will never forgive me. She certainly won't want me for a roommate anymore."

Rachel was waiting when Cindy got home from the track that afternoon. "I've decided to move in with Matt," Rachel announced. "And I'm sorry about what I said to you, Cindy. I know you're only doing what you have to do."

Cindy nodded slowly. "Are you sure you're not mad at me?" she asked.

"I couldn't stay mad," Rachel said, giving Cindy a bright smile. "If it hadn't been for you, I probably never would have gotten to know Matt."

Within a few days Rachel had her things moved out of the apartment. The first thing Cindy did was to move her bedroom furniture into the bigger bedroom. The bed and dresser, which had filled the closet-sized room, seemed lost in the larger room. After she was done moving, Cindy wandered through the quiet apartment, which felt strangely empty. "Maybe I need a cat," she said, then promptly dismissed the thought. It would be nice to have a pet around when she wanted companionship, but it wouldn't be fair for the animal to spend so much time alone. Besides, she reminded herself, she was home so little that she couldn't even keep a house plant alive. She would just have to be satisfied with the hours she spent every day around the horses at the track.

When the phone rang later, she was happy to hear Ian's voice. "How are things in New York?" he asked, sounding cheerful.

"Hi, Dad." Cindy sat down on the sofa and curled her feet under her. "What's going on?"

"Beth and I thought we would take a few days of vacation and come for a visit," her father said. "Kevin is so excited about going to New York."

"When are you coming?" Cindy asked.

"We were thinking next weekend might be good," Ian said.

"Great," Cindy said, trying to sound sincere. Phoenix's race was the next weekend as well. She wanted to see her family, but she wasn't so sure she wanted the added pressure of having her family there to watch her race. Ian might not be too pleased to see her riding an unsound horse in a claiming race, after all her talk about how well she was doing. "I'm racing on Saturday," she said.

"Perfect," Ian said enthusiastically. "It's been a while since we saw you race. I'm looking forward to it."

"It'll be nice to have all of you here," Cindy said.

"Kevin will be thrilled," her father said. "It's been a long time since he's seen his big sister, and we can all stand at the rail and cheer you on."

Cindy smiled to herself, feeling better. Ian would never criticize the horses she rode. He and Beth would be happy that she was doing what she loved. She didn't have to prove anything to them. And it would be nice to know she had her own cheering section while she and Phoenix were racing.

"I'm excited about seeing all of you," she said, her enthusiasm sincere this time. "It'll be great to have you here."

When Cindy hung up the phone, she noticed that her shoulder was starting to ache. Probably from moving the furniture by herself, she thought. She took some aspirin and went to bed, sure that it would be fine in the morning. But it continued to bother her for the next couple of days, and she found herself limiting what she did with it. She wasn't going to get pulled from the race because of a little stiffness in her shoulder. She had to be in good shape for Phoenix.

Friday afternoon she waited eagerly for Ian and Beth to arrive. The apartment was neat and tidy. The window with its dreary view was sparkling, and Cindy had arranged fresh flowers in water glasses, placing them around the apartment to brighten it up. She gazed around the living room, satisfied that the little place was clean and inviting.

When her parents walked in the door, she was anxious to see how they'd react.

"This is really cute," Beth said, walking into the living room. She stuck her head around the corner to look into the kitchen. "What a nice, efficient work area," she said approvingly.

Ian sat down on the sofa and leaned back. "This is a lot nicer than anything I lived in when I was your age," he said, looking around and nodding. "You seem to be doing pretty well for yourself."

Cindy breathed a sigh of relief. So far, so good.

Soon they were involved in conversation about the horses at Whitebrook, Cindy's work at the track, Samantha and Tor's new life in Ireland, and the fact that Kevin would soon be starting first grade.

Cindy left for the track early the next morning after giving Ian and Beth Phoenix's stall location. She arrived at the backside gate and paused to look around. Everything there was so familiar now. She had been walking up to the back gate every day for a year. Cindy realized she was very much at home at Belmont. The security guard gave her a friendly wave, and

Cindy smiled at the man, greeting him as she strode through the gate.

She met up with Matt as she was heading for the jockeys' lounge to check over her equipment.

"You realize that the odds against that filly are astronomical," Matt said, stopping her outside the door.

"I know," Cindy said. "But I'm still going to ride her like she's a winner."

"I wish I could say I hope you do win," Matt said. "But I really want Falcon and Rachel to beat you."

"I understand," Cindy said with a smile. She held her hand out to Matt. "Good luck with Falcon."

Matt shook her hand firmly. "You take care out there," he said.

"I will," Cindy said. "Thanks, Matt."

After reassuring herself that her tack was in perfect order, Cindy went to work, exercising several horses for different trainers. After the morning works ended, she went to Phoenix's stall. The filly whinnied excitedly, as though she sensed the prerace tension in the air.

The groom assigned to the filly walked up as Cindy opened the stall door. "I'll have her groomed and ready for you before the race," he said.

Cindy smiled at the groom. "Thanks," she said. "But I'll take care of Phoenix today."

When he started to protest, she shook her head,

smiling. "It's all right. I want to." She patted the filly's neck affectionately. This was the last time she would be bathing the filly, wrapping her legs, or taking her onto the track. She wanted to make sure Phoenix looked perfect for her race.

"Okay," the groom said reluctantly, and walked away.

Cindy bathed Phoenix thoroughly, laughing at the way the filly arched her neck when the water ran down her back. "You're going to be awesome today," she said, scrubbing shampoo into Phoenix's shoulder. "I know you are. I wish I had the money to put in a claim on you myself. Now that you're sound, all you need is a little more time to get used to racing."

Phoenix flicked her ears and stamped her hind foot, reminding Cindy that she wasn't finished with her grooming.

Once Phoenix's mane and tail were combed smooth and her glossy coat was dry, Cindy brushed the filly until her coat shone in the sunshine, then wrapped her legs carefully.

"We're going to be fine," she said softly, as much to herself as the filly. "You won't have any problems at all, will you? You're going to make Mrs. Goldrich sorry she decided to sell you off."

The filly looked at her with keen, bright eyes, and

Cindy nodded. "You're going to make those odds-makers look pretty silly," she said, draping a blanket over the filly's back.

She put Phoenix in her stall and went in search of Lonnie, in case the trainer had a few last-minute words of advice for her.

"Cindy!"

She saw Ian and Beth coming along the shed row toward her, Kevin between them.

"Where is this filly you're riding today?" Ian asked, gazing curiously around the GeeGee stables. His attention settled on one of the top horses in the stable. "They certainly have some good-looking horses here."

"This is Phoenix," Cindy said, gesturing toward the filly's stall. The chestnut filly dropped her head to sniff Kevin's hair.

"She looks like a nice little filly," Ian said.

"She is," Cindy said, then blurted out her misgivings about riding the filly. "She seems sound now, but I'm afraid she might get hurt," she said, leaving out that she was worried about her own shoulder, too. "And if we don't do well, I'm afraid of what will happen to her."

Ian looked at Phoenix again, then turned to Cindy. "What's your instinct telling you to do with her?" he asked.

Cindy glanced at Phoenix and thought back to all their works on the track. "I need to do everything I can to get her to the rail, get her in front, and just let her run," she said. "She's really fast, Dad. But I don't want to stress her leg by taking her wide."

Ian nodded. "You'll do fine," he said, giving Cindy's confidence a huge boost. "You know the track, you know this horse, and you know how to read the field." He clapped his hand on Cindy's shoulder. "And no matter how you do today, as long as you've done your best, you can walk off the track with your head high."

"Thanks, Dad," Cindy said, confidence blooming inside her. She knew how to read her horse and how to manage a difficult field. Ian was right. She just needed to listen to her instincts. Suddenly Cindy felt relieved of the pressure she had been putting on herself. She was a good jockey, and she'd show everyone how well she could ride a good horse.

When it was time for Cindy to go to the jockeys' lounge to weigh in and change into her silks, Beth gave her a quick hug. "Good luck, sweetheart," she said. "We'll be the loudest people at the rail."

"Thanks, Mom," Cindy said gratefully, tears of gratitude springing to her eyes.

"We'll see you trackside," Ian said, waving goodbye as they headed for the track kitchen to have lunch before the races started.

Cindy changed quickly and waited tensely in the lounge for her race to come up. When Rachel walked out of the locker room wearing Stone Ridge's silks, their eyes met.

Rachel gave her a thin smile. "Good luck," she said, looking nervous.

"You too, Rachel," Cindy said, standing up to join the jockeys heading for the viewing paddock. She walked beside Rachel, her saddle draped over her arm, but they didn't speak during the long walk through the tunnel. When they reached the saddling area, Matt took Rachel's saddle and gave Cindy a brief nod. She flashed him a quick smile and handed her racing saddle to Lonnie, then headed for the viewing paddock to wait for the groom to lead Phoenix in.

There was a well-dressed young woman waiting at Phoenix's gate number when Cindy walked across the ring. She turned to Cindy and smiled. "So you're the jockey who's been trying to save my aunt Gloria's filly," she said, holding out her hand. "My name is Linda Owen. Lonnie thought it would be nice if someone was here to represent Aunt Gloria in case you win today. Besides," she said, "I've always thought there was something special about Phoenix. I wanted to come cheer her on."

Cindy was delighted. She had been under the impression that Lonnie didn't care at all about whether Phoenix won or lost. She shook Linda's hand, smiling enthusiastically. "I hope we see you in the winner's circle," she said.

When the handler brought Phoenix around, Cindy sprang lightly onto her back, and soon they were heading for the gate at the far corner of the track.

Phoenix danced impatiently behind the gate, waiting for their turn to be loaded. They had drawn the number five position, so once again they were in the middle of the pack, but Cindy wasn't going to let Phoenix get bunched in again. Falcon had drawn the number seven slot, only one horse away. Cindy glanced at Rachel, but her friend was staring straight ahead. Cindy turned back to the track and inhaled and exhaled deeply, trying to focus on the view between Phoenix's pricked ears.

The starting gate opened with a clang. Phoenix dove onto the track, and Cindy immediately drove her toward the rail. The only horse in front of them was the number two horse, and Cindy brought Phoenix to the outside, determined to get in front of the pack. She would not let the slower horses keep the filly from running her best.

A quick glance under her arm showed Cindy that

the pack of horses was right behind them, the jockeys and horses struggling for good positions. She saw Falcon far on the outside, and she grimaced. Rachel was making a mistake by taking Falcon wide. The filly was fast, but she wasn't a distance horse, and staying on the outside meant she was running farther than the rest of the horses in the field. But Cindy couldn't worry about that. She leaned over Phoenix's shoulders and urged her on.

As they came into the turn she could hear the deep breathing of the horses on both sides of them. Phoenix's muscles strained as she ran, striving to get ahead of the number two horse.

They came onto the straight stretch and galloped on, Phoenix giving her all with little urging from Cindy. The filly wanted to run, and she wanted to win. To Cindy's relief, Phoenix was running strongly, her strides powerful and long, showing no sign of weakness.

Cindy balanced over her withers and encouraged the filly to keep running. "Come on, girl," she cried, feeling the surge of energy as Phoenix dug in deeper. The number two horse slipped back to their hip, and Cindy swallowed a whoop of elation. The race wasn't over yet, but it looked as though no one was going to touch them!

Then she felt the pounding hooves of a horse coming up on their right, and she darted a glance over to see Rachel and Falcon shooting up beside them. For a few seconds the two chestnut fillies were neck and neck, battling down to the wire for first place. But Phoenix seemed to have nothing extra left, and as they came down to the finish line, Falcon surged forward and crossed it a head in front of Phoenix.

Cindy slowed the galloping filly and finally brought her back around to where the handler was waiting. She hopped from Phoenix's back as Lonnie came onto the track. The trainer ran his hand down the filly's leg, then looked up at Cindy.

"She held up fine," he said, smiling.

"Great," Cindy said, wishing she didn't feel so sad. "I'm sure her new owners will be pleased."

"I am," a familiar voice said. Cindy turned quickly to see Linda Owen standing by the rail. "I didn't want to tell you before you raced, but I decided to have Lonnie place a claim on her for me. He told me earlier today how much work you've done with her and what kind of progress she's made. I believe my aunt wasn't thinking clearly when she decided to sell Phoenix. Lonnie has agreed to continue to train her for me."

Cindy wished she could throw her arms around Linda, but instead she settled for a huge smile. "That's wonderful," she said, ecstatic about Phoenix's good luck. She turned to the filly. "You're going to be fine," she said, patting her sweaty neck.

"As long as she stays sound, we'll run her a few more times," Lonnie said as Cindy dragged the saddle off Phoenix's back. "Once she's got a decent lifetime winnings record, we'll retire her to the breeding farm. Does that make you happy?"

Cindy beamed at the trainer. "You know it does," she said.

"I hope you'll keep racing her for us," Linda said.

Cindy nodded. "I'd love to," she said.

Lonnie led Phoenix off, and Cindy glanced toward the winner's circle, where Matt and Rachel were posing with Falcon. Her happy mood faded. Falcon might have won the race, but if someone claimed her, Matt would lose the best horse he owned.

"Cindy!" Beth waved to her from the rail, and Cindy walked over to where Beth, Ian, and Kevin waited.

"We'll meet you at the backside," Ian said. "As soon as you're ready to go, we're taking you out to a victory dinner."

"But we didn't win," Cindy protested.

"Maybe not, but you were great out there today," Ian said, smiling proudly.

"Thanks," Cindy said. "I'll see you as soon as I change."

She met up with Rachel as she headed for the backside. "Congratulations," she said. "That was a great race."

"You too," Rachel said. "I was afraid we weren't going to pull it off. Your filly had a lot more drive than I expected."

"I'm sorry Matt decided to sell Falcon," Cindy said.

Rachel shrugged. "No one claimed her," she said, smiling. "We've decided to keep her anyway. We won't have much money for a while, but we'll be okay."

"I know you will," Cindy said. "You and Matt are perfect for each other."

"Thanks," Rachel said. Instead of going to the jockeys' lounge, Rachel headed for the veterinarian's barn to see Matt and Falcon. Cindy continued on to the jockeys' quarters, feeling lighthearted. She had saved Phoenix, and after Ian had reminded her to listen to herself, she knew she'd be fine. Her confidence was back, and she was full of hope for the future.

After a festive celebration dinner with her family, Cindy went to bed still smiling over the way the day had turned out. She opened her diary and leaned back against the headboard to make one more entry in the little book.

Phoenix is safe, and I know now that I am going to reach my goal of being a successful jockey. I have my confidence back, thanks to Dad reminding me that I have good instincts and that I'm a good jockey in my own right. I'm still going to have to work hard, but now I know it's worth the effort. Finally I feel like I'm on the right track!

13

RRRING! RRRING!

The sound of the phone made Cindy jump. She scrambled to her feet and glanced at the clock beside the bed. She had been sitting on the floor reading through her old diary for nearly two hours! She gave her head a quick shake, trying to clear her mind of all the memories before she answered the phone.

"Hello?"

"This is Phyllis from A to Z Movers," the woman on the line said. "We're confirming your appointment for tomorrow morning."

Cindy set the book aside and spent a few minutes going over the arrangements with the moving company.

After she hung up the phone, she rushed through

the apartment. She didn't have time for any more trips down memory lane. She spent the next several hours packing her things into the waiting boxes. She took a short break to grab a slice of take-out pizza, then went back to work, sorting through the things she had accumulated in the last twelve years. It was almost midnight when she finally stood back from the mountain of boxes stacked in the living room, ready for the moving company to carry out to their van. Her back ached from all the bending and carrying, but she had a good sense of accomplishment. Exhausted, she crawled into bed and fell asleep immediately, barely stirring until she woke up the next morning to the incessant buzzing of her alarm.

"How did I manage to sleep so late?" she groaned, reaching over to shut off the alarm. "I need to get to the track." She sat up, still fuzzy-headed, but one look around the bare room brought her back to reality. Five o'clock workouts at Belmont were no longer a part of her life.

Pensively she wriggled her left shoulder. It felt okay, even after all the work she had done the day before. Maybe she could still ride after all. She ran her hand along the scar that marked her skin from the surgery. "Forget it," she told herself. "There isn't a race in the world worth crippling yourself for." It was time to move on.

Cindy rose, dressed, and finished packing the few things that were left. By the time the movers arrived, she was ready to close up the apartment and leave New York for good. She gave the driver directions to Tall Oaks and watched the moving van pull away from the curb, loaded with her possessions. Then she got into her own car and drove away from the city that had been the center of her life for more than a decade.

After spending the night in a motel in Charleston, West Virginia, Cindy drove on to Lexington, heading straight for Tall Oaks, and arriving at the estate early in the afternoon. She parked under a budding oak tree that grew in front of the guest house, near the sprawling barns. She climbed from the car and gazed at the quaint cottage that was to be her new home. Even though it was tiny compared to Tall Oaks' colonial-style main house, the guest house was several times larger than the New York apartment. Cindy looked forward to furnishing it and making it into a pleasant home.

As soon as she had a table and chairs, she would invite her family to dinner. She smiled at the idea of playing hostess. Maybe Beth could give her a few cooking lessons.

Cindy started toward the house, eager to unload the boxes she had brought down in her car while she waited for the moving van to arrive. When she saw Fredericka walking down from the main house, Cindy waited for the older woman. As she got closer, Cindy could see that Fredericka's expression was serious.

Fredericka stopped beside Cindy's car and smiled weakly. "It's lovely to see you," she said, her voice sounding strained. "I hope your trip went smoothly."

"It was fine," Cindy said. She frowned. "Is there a problem?"

Fredericka nodded slowly, and Cindy felt her heart sink. "Is it because of Alexis again?"

Alexis, the former Tall Oaks farm manager, had taken advantage of Fredericka's trust and had bought extremely high-priced horses for Tall Oaks based on the size of the commissions she received, not on what was best for the farm. Fredericka's sole concern was the well-being of her beloved Thoroughbreds, and she had paid little attention to the financial end of the business until she found herself in serious debt. Cindy had worked with her to find good buyers for some of her horses, but she had convinced Fredericka to keep Khan, her best stallion, and Gratis, the bay colt who was in training for the Kentucky Derby, as well as a few mares for breeding stock.

"I truly believed selling some of the stock would be enough to solve my financial problems," Fredericka said. "But it wasn't enough."

"I thought you could hang on until Gratis raced in one of the Championship series races," Cindy said. The series helped sort out which horses would run in the Kentucky Derby, the Preakness, and the Belmont, the three prestigious races that made up the Triple Crown. "If Gratis is running well, he should bring in some big purses before long. And breeding season is starting up soon. Khan's stud fees will help turn things around."

Fredericka shook her head sadly. "It's too late, Cindy."

Cindy felt her hopes for the future shatter. While she had been struggling to accept the loss of her career as a jockey, the thought of working for Fredericka had given her something to focus on. The idea of having her own little house at Tall Oaks and caring for quality horses on a nice farm had kept her spirits up. Most of all, she had looked forward to working under Vince Jones, learning what made him one of the top trainers at the track year after year.

"I got a call yesterday from a friend who is a real estate agent," Fredericka said. "He has someone who wants to buy Tall Oaks as it is, horses and all."

"But you can't sell Khan or Gratis!" Cindy cried.

Fredericka looked at the ground. "The buyer is coming today to sign the papers. He has the money to pay cash for everything."

"But what will you do without Tall Oaks?" Cindy demanded.

Fredericka sighed. "I will miss living here, of course, but I talked to my daughter last night. She agreed that the estate has become too much of a burden for me. I've decided to move to California to live near my daughter and grandchildren." She smiled sadly. "I am sorry, Cindy. I know you had hopes for Tall Oaks' future, too."

"But Tall Oaks has been in the Graber family since the Civil War," Cindy protested. "You can't just sell it."

"The new buyer has agreed to keep everything as it is. Tall Oaks won't change, Cindy. The estate will remain intact, and the new owner has the funds to maintain everything to the highest standards. I made certain that was in the contract."

"I understand," Cindy said quietly. "I'll wait here until the moving van arrives. Then I'll have them take my things to a storage unit."

"Oh, no!" Fredericka exclaimed. "You still have a job here."

"I'm sure the new owner will want to hire his or her own trainer," Cindy said. "I don't expect to be guaranteed a job."

Fredericka rested a hand on Cindy's arm. "The buyer was very specific that he wanted you to stay on as the farm manager."

"He wanted me? But he doesn't know me," Cindy said, baffled by the mysterious buyer's request. "I'm not sure I understand."

The sound of a vehicle coming up the drive distracted Fredericka. She pointed behind Cindy. "The buyer can explain it all himself," she said. "He's here now."

Cindy turned to see a black limousine roll to a stop near Cindy's car. She stared, disbelieving, as Ben al-Rihani climbed from the vehicle.

Cindy gaped at the tall, handsome horse owner from Dubai. "Ben? Wh-what are you doing here?" she stammered.

"I'm here to sign some documents with Mrs. Graber," Ben said, smiling brilliantly.

Fredericka smiled back at Ben, her expression brightening. "Mr. al-Rihani is buying Tall Oaks," she said, sounding relieved.

"You?" Cindy's jaw worked as she struggled to absorb the news.

"It makes more sense to have a facility here than to buy horses and ship them to the United Arab Emirates for training," Ben said reasonably. "I find myself spending an increasing amount of time in the United States and far less in Dubai. I love the green fields of Kentucky, and the mansion here is the kind of house I've always wanted." He gave Fredericka a warm look.

"And I will treat it with the respect and care it deserves as a piece of American history."

"I need to go back up to the main house," Fredericka said, looking at Cindy. "I will leave you and Mr. al-Rihani to work out your employment arrangements." She smiled fondly at Ben. "My attorney should be here shortly," she said. "I'll meet you up at the house when you're ready."

Fredericka walked away, leaving Cindy and Ben standing in front of the little guest house.

Cindy stared at Ben, still trying to comprehend what was going on. "You're buying Tall Oaks?" she said incredulously.

He nodded. "That is what the contract says," he replied. "But I am buying it with the understanding that you will stay on as the trainer."

Cindy shook her head. "I can't do that," she said stiffly.

"Why not?" Ben asked. "Everything will be the way you and Mrs. Graber agreed. You'll have the cottage, you'll be working with Vince Jones to train Gratis, and you'll be in charge of the barns."

"I will not work for the al-Rihanis again," Cindy said sharply. "I made that mistake once, Ben. I won't do it again."

"You are still angry over the conversation you heard between my father and me, aren't you?" Ben asked.

Cindy looked away from him. "That was a long time ago," she said stiffly. "It doesn't matter anymore."

"It does to me," Ben said. "You only heard me being sarcastic. I was repeating what he had just said to me. I would never turn on you like that."

Cindy slowly turned to look at him again. "You stood up to your father for me?"

Ben shrugged. "It was high time I did," he said. "He didn't speak to me for a long time, but then he got over it, and even admitted he'd been wrong about you."

Cindy stared at Ben, her jaw slack, too stunned to speak.

"Now," he said, clapping his hands, "about that job . . ."

Cindy shook her head again, looking down at the ground. "I just don't know," she said.

Ben frowned. "You leave me no choice, then," he said grimly.

"What?" Cindy demanded.

"If you won't work for me, will you work with me?"

Cindy stared at him, confused. "You mean as partners?"

Ben nodded. "That's exactly what I mean," he said. "With your horse skills and experience, we could rebuild the horse business at Tall Oaks into a top-notch stable. You'd be a partner in the business, not an employee. What do you say?"

Cindy considered the offer, then folded her arms across her chest. "On one condition," she said finally.

"And what would that be?" Ben asked.

"That you bring Champion back to Kentucky where he belongs," Cindy said, sure she was asking for the one thing Ben couldn't give her.

To her amazement, Ben started to laugh. "That was going to be my final bribe to get you to stay," he said. "I've already made the arrangements. Champion will be standing stud at Tall Oaks when the breeding season starts again."

Cindy clapped her hands to her mouth and gasped. Then she threw herself at Ben, flinging her arms around his neck, not sure whether she should laugh or cry. She stepped back and looked up at him. "You're really bringing Champion home?"

Ben nodded smugly. "Absolutely. Now, if you want to walk through the barns and make a list of what you would like to see done right away, I'll go up and sign those papers with Mrs. Graber."

He returned to the waiting limousine. Cindy watched the car drive on up to the main house, then turned to eye the stately barns. "First things first," she said to herself. "I need to make sure the best stall in the barn is fixed up for Champion." With a firm nod,

Cindy headed for the stallion barn, not sure if she was walking on the ground or floating on air. After all these years, she and Champion were both going to be where they belonged—at home in Kentucky, with their whole lives ahead of them.

MARY NEWHALL ANDERSON spent her childhood exploring back roads and trails on horseback with her best friend. She now lives with her husband, her horse-crazy daughter, Danielle, and five horses on Washington State's Olympic Peninsula. Mary has published novels and short stories for both adults and young adults.